# Mi Latina

## The Bloody Romance

by

King Tremayne

**DORRANCE**
PUBLISHING CO
EST. 1920
PITTSBURGH, PENNSYLVANIA 15238

The contents of this work, including, but not limited to, the accuracy of events, people, and places depicted; opinions expressed; permission to use previously published materials included; and any advice given or actions advocated are solely the responsibility of the author, who assumes all liability for said work and indemnifies the publisher against any claims stemming from publication of the work.

Dorrance Publishing Co
585 Alpha Drive
Suite 103
Pittsburgh, PA 15238
Visit our website at www.dorrancebookstore.com

ISBN: 978-1-4809-4685-9
eISBN: 978-1-4809-4662-0

# *Introduction:*
# *Humble Beginnings*

ACT 1 - SCENE 1

Chicago, IL. May 13, 1978. Cook County Hospital.

Fifteen-year-old Brittany Davis, legs raised, screams in pain as she gives birth with her mother holding her hand, coaxing her through the pain and pushes.

#### Doctor:

Brittany, you're almost there. I'm going to need you to give me at least two or three more big pushes, okay?!

#### Brittany:

(through tears) Okay!

#### Doctor:

Okay, on three. One, two…

She pushes, causing her bowels to violently spew defecation in the doctor's face and chest.

Doctor:

Not quite what I was expecting, but, the head is out.

The baby's cries fill the room.

Doctor:

One more should do it. On three, one, two…

Brittany takes a deep breath, bears down, and grunts, pushing with all of the force she can muster. The doctor raises the baby, handing it to a nurse to be cleaned.

Doctor:

It's a boy. Now, if you ladies'll excuse me, I'll make my exit to clean myself.

Brittany:

I'm so sorry, Doctor.

Doctor:

Don't worry about it. It's perfectly natural. You don't deliver babies as long as I have, without occasionally getting sprayed.

The room goes up in a fit of laughter as the doctor asks Bernadette, Brittany's mother, if she'd like to cut the cord.

Doctor:

Would you like to do the honors, Bernie?

Bernadette squeals as she nervously approaches her newborn grandson.

Bernadette:

I'm so nervous.

Bernadette takes the medical scissors as the nurse guides her through the process. She makes the cut.

Doctor:

And there it is. Have you thought of a name, yet?

Brittany:

Steven Marcus Davis.


Dialog in Spanish-Scene 2: Cali, Colombia. May 13, 1978.

Sylvia's screams are heard outside of her hovel of a home. Three men are not ten feet away, moving back and forth in a hybrid kitchen/living room, packing pure cocaine into kilos. Cristobal assists his wife while she writhes in pain on the floor. His brother, Don, looks on a kilo.

Cristobal:

(screaming at Don) HELP ME, HERMANO, HELP ME!!!

Don:

One minute, what do you need?

Sylvia's screams jar the men into attention, causing Ramon, her brother, to tease her.

Ramon:

Hermana, shut up, already. We're trying to pack kilos over here!

Sylvia:

You shut up, asshole! I'm giving birth to your niece over here, help me!!!

Ramon:

(gets up and makes his way to his sister with cocaine-covered hands) Look, hermana, I brought you some cocaine to help take the edge off.

Ramon laughs at this, by himself, as Cristobal and Sylvia both curse him for joking at a time like this.

Cristobal:

Fucking asshole! Go wash your hands!

Sylvia:

You're lucky you're my brother!

Ramon rises, sniffing cocaine from the backs of his hands as he makes his way to thoroughly clean them. Don approaches with a bucket of water and a sheet.

Cristobal:

(to Sylvia) One more big push, bella. One more, one, two…

Sylvia strains as the baby exits her womb. Don looks at Sylvia.

Don:

She's so precious, so pretty.

Cristobal:

(through tears) Mi hija, Mi hija. (My daughter.)

Sylvia:

(raising her a head, trying to see) Let me see my baby, Cristobal.

Ramon cleans the baby as Cristobal pours tequila on his knife and cuts the umbilical cord.

Cristobal:

One minute, mi amor, we're almost done cleaning her.

Don:

What's her name, cunada? (sister-in-law)

Sylvia:

Sonrisa Ciela Jerez.

Don:

Heaven's Smile. Beautiful.

Cristobal wraps Sonrisa in a sheet and gently beams at his daughter. Cristobal looks momentarily at the baby's forehead and runs into the kitchen as Ramon comes in with clean hands.

Ramon:

What happened?!

Sylvia:

Come and kiss your niece, that's what happened!

Ramon rushes to his sister and newborn niece, kissing Sonrisa's forehead.

Ramon:

She's so pretty. Unlike her mother.

He laughs at his own joke as Sylvia swats at him. He kisses her cheek, saying as he goes into the kitchen…

Ramon:

Why so mean, hermana? You just had your first child.

Sylvia:

Shut up, you idiot! (to Sonrisa) Your uncle is stupid, mi amor.

At the table, the four men argue.

Ricardo:

Hurry up!

Don:

Just do your job.

The door is kicked open, and a roar of gunshots from two AK-47s sends a barrage of bullets into the four men at the table, causing blood and cocaine to spray everywhere. Sylvia's screams and Sonrisa's muffled cries fill the room as the gunmen stop firing upon realizing the four men need no further assistance in dying. One calls back.

Man #1

Don Jefe, it's clear, Vibora.

Twenty-year-old Don Jefe enters the room, stepping through, splitting his bodyguards. He purposely ignores the four clearly dead men in the kitchen, immediately approaching the crying Sylvia and her wailing daughter.

Vibora:

Calm down, Sylvia, calm down. (He snaps his fingers and points, signaling to the men to check the rest of the house.) Did you have a boy or a girl?

Sylvia:

A girl.

Vibora:

Congratulations, can I see her?

Sylvia:

Please, Vibora, don't hurt her. I just had her not five minutes ago.

Vibora:

Calm down, chiquita. I have a soft spot for beautiful women.

Sylvia hands Sonrisa to Vibora.

Vibora:

She's so precious.

Sylvia:

Gracias, Don Jefe.

The two bodyguards enter the room.

Man #2:

It's clear, Don Jefe.

Man #1:

Do you want us to grab the rest of the cocaine?

Vibora:

Si, whatever can be saved. (to Sylvia) Besides, these two ladies will spend the rest of their lives paying Sylvia's husband's and their brothers' debt. (to Sonrisa as he lightly bounces her as she cries) Calma, nina, calma. You're safe now. (to Sylvia) What's her name?

Sylvia:

Sonrisa Ciela.

Vibora:

Heaven's Smile. Beautiful. (He kisses Sonrisa.)

Scene 3-May 13, 1993. Humboldt Park, Chicago, IL. Northside.

Daddy Yankee ft. Snoop Dogg-Gangsta' Zone plays throughout the scene as a freshly turned fifteen-year-old Steven spends his birthday thus; he and six friends pass blunts and a fifth of tequila around their circle. Three in the crowd are black, the other three Latino.

Juan:

(in Spanish to Steven) Happy Birthday, carnal.

Steve:

Gracias.

Bobby:

Okay, it's his birthday, get over it. Don't fuck this up or it'll be his last.

The entire group pulls ski masks from their pants pockets and dons them.

Pelon:

Me and Juan will take the main floor, Steve and Bobby go downstairs, Tiny, Greg, and Joker, go upstairs.

Greg:

And, please, don't kill any kids.

All of the men pull either Tec 9s, .9mms, or .45 autos from their hips.

Meanwhile, an overhead view of the house reveals two rooms. In the room to the left, two couples are engaged in sexual intercourse in one bed. One is in the doggy-style position, while the lady next to them straddles her lover. Kids play in the room on the right.

On the main floor, drugs are being cooked and/or mixed in the kitchen, while five men in the living room package drugs as they count and bundle money. Five drug addicts are in the basement, two are unconscious with needles dangling from their forearms, and one nods while standing up, while the three who remain smoke rocks.

The front door bursts open, and before the people in the room can react they're quickly mowed down while five men run toward the kitchen and the other two run upstairs.

In the kitchen, the cook catches four shots to the body, while the man closest to the entrance takes two to the face. The third man reaches all too slowly and is shot in the head.

Upstairs, the man and woman who are in the controlling sexual positions take headshots, which splatter blood and brain matter onto their lovers. The two on the bottom both turn, tossing the corpses from on top of them, only to be greeted by two gunshots to the head apiece. Behind them they hear a door creak open, and a little girl stares at the two masked men. One of them approaches her while placing his gun down his spine, and the other immediately starts searching the room for any weapons, money, and/or drugs. He kneels down and tells the little girl…

Masked Man:

Go back in the room and don't come back out, okay?

The little girl nods in the affirmative and closes the door.

Scene 4-May 13, 1993, Cali, Colombia.

Sonrisa Ciela Jerez turns fifteen today; the only catch is that she turns fifteen in a whorehouse, where she was raised and where her mother has worked every day since her father and uncles were murdered fifteen years ago to the day.

She is awakened by the sound of a lone gunshot. Scared, she runs to her mother's room. She opens the door, calling (dialogue in Spanish)...

Sonrisa:

Mama, it's my birthday...

She screams upon seeing her mother's body sprawled on the bed, blood running from the gaping hole left by the self-inflicted gunshot wound to the head. She runs to her mother's body, cradling her head and crying to the ceiling to bring her mother back.

Sonrisa:

GOD, PLEASE DON'T TAKE MY MOTHER, PLEASE?!!!!

Whores, their dates, and the Madame, Gigi, all come to Sylvia's room. Gigi fans the crowd away.

Gigi:

Go back to your rooms, hurry, hurry!

She walks quickly to Sonrisa, pulling her away from her mother's corpse. Sonrisa pulls away, reaching for her mother, crying loudly.

Gigi:

Sonrisa, calm down, sweetheart, calm down. You shouldn't have to see this.

Sonrisa never stops crying as Gigi drags her from her mother's room.

Two hours later: On her bunk bed, Sonrisa cries as Don Jefe enters the room and sits next to her.

Vibora:

Sonrisa, my condolences in regards to your mother. I'm very sorry.

All of Sonrisa's bottled-up hatred toward this man begins to simmer as she speaks, barely holding in her ire.

Sonrisa:

Gracias, Vibora. But we both know that you never cared for me and my mother.

Vibora:

That's not true, pretty one. If I didn't care for you and your mother, you'd've died on this day fifteen years ago.

She looks at him in shock, not believing he remembered the initial horror he inflicted on her family the first day she was born. And now, on her fifteenth birthday, her mother dies. The hits just keep coming.

Vibora:

Don't look so surprised, pequena. Happy Birthday.

Sonrisa:

How could you forget slaughtering my family like pigs right after I was born?!

Vibora:

(remaining calm) Because of your loss today, I'm going to allow your disrespectful tone toward me. I could've left you and your mother in that hut that I burned to the ground and watched you two burn to death. But I let you live. No one told your father and uncles to steal from my father, but they did. You and your mother were not to blame, but there's a price to pay for such things.

She explodes in his face.

Sonrisa:

Now that my mother's dead, how long do I have to be a whore for what my father did to your father?!

He slaps her twice.

Vibora:

How dare you speak to me in this way! You'll work for me until I say you can go.

Sonrisa:

You've had me doing this ever since I bled when I turned twelve! You're a monster.

She spits in his face.

Vibora:

And today's no different, chiquitita. In respect for your mother, I'll let you have her room after we put a new bed in it. (He pulls a handkerchief from his pocket and wipes his face clean.) Think of it as an inheritance. And I think she left you some presents for your fifteenth birthday. It's a special time in a Latina's life, her fifteenth birthday. Maybe not for you, but for many other girls whose fathers didn't steal from drug lords or who were lucky enough not to run away from home and get strung out, kidnapped, or both. She has a big Quinceañera, gets lots of presents, money, wears a pretty dress, dances with her father.... Oh, wait.... (He grins devilishly at a teary-eyed Sonrisa.) I almost forgot, you don't have a father, and as of today you have no mother. (He mocks her by tilting his head and pursing his bottom lip.) Happy Birthday, pretty one.

She rushes him, slapping him hard across the cheek. He only smiles.

Vibora:

Remember your first period? You were twelve and tight, sweet. I wanted so badly to lick you down there, pretty one, before I started selling you. Now I can never lick you there, how sad for the both of us, pretty one. Gigi will show you my gift to you in a while. And even though you don't believe me, I am truly sorry for your loss. In spite of everything, I always liked your mother.

One hour later: Sonrisa stares blankly into a mirror at her reflection as Gigi puts the finishing touches on her makeup. Don Jefe's words cut through her mind like a sword through water as the image of her mother's corpse is vivid in her mind.

Vibora's Voiceover:

It's a special day in a Latina's life, her fifteenth birthday.... She has a Quinceañera, gets lots of presents, money, wears a pretty dress, dances with her father.... Oh, wait.... (His face blends with the image of her mother's corpse.) I almost forgot, you don't have a father. And, as of today, you don't have a mother.... (His voice echoes out.)

A tear rolls down her cheek, slightly agitating Gigi, who quickly dabs it dry before it can ruin her makeup.

Gigi:

No, amiga, you have to stop crying. You have to entertain. I know it's hard, but you're all you have now.

Meanwhile, four men wait in a bedroom, all clad in nothing but their underwear, when the door opens, revealing Sonrisa, young and beautiful. Meat being thrown to a wolf pack.

She enters the room slowly, gently closing the door behind her. The men waste no time in undressing her, exposing her breasts and shaved pubic area. One man lies on his back as another takes down her panties. She steps into bed, straddling the man who's on his back, gasping as he penetrates her straightaway. The man behind her pulls her ponytail, causing her head to go back as the third man forces his penis into her mouth. The man who's behind her slowly forces his way into her anus, making her eyes widen as she inadvertently bites down on the member in her mouth. The man yells and pulls out of her mouth, slapping her and cursing.

Male:

Fucking whore bit my dick!!!

The other men laugh at his pain as the fourth man places his erection into

Sonrisa's mouth as tears leave her eyes.

Male #2:

Don't bite me, bitch!

The man in her anus thrusts into her harder and harder as he releases his load into her rectum. The man she bit enters her behind roughly, revenge-pumping for the bite she gave him. The man receiving fellatio pulls out after shooting half of his load into her mouth, releasing the rest of his fluid into her eyes and face. The man she rides shakes in ecstasy as he emits semen into her. He slides from beneath her as the man behind her pounds away. She puts her face into the pillow, wipes as much sperm from it as she can, and mumbles a soft prayer to herself and her god.

Sonrisa:

Please, God, help me?! Send me someone to rescue me from this hell that I was born into, please? I don't deserve this. What did I do to deserve this?

She wears a defiant look as tears roll down her cheeks.

Scene 5-Humboldt Park. Chicago, IL. November 13, 2007.

Steve and Bobby sit on Steve's front porch, smoking a joint and drinking bottled beers.

Bobby:

So, you're leaving The City, huh? Yo' ass'll be back.

Steve:

Never. I gotta feelin' that when I leave I'll stay where I am.

Bobby:

Why now?

Steve:

We too damn old to be still playin' robbers and robbers with these goddamn Latinos out here. They don't stop. They take this gangbangin' shit way mo' serious than we do. They got forty- and fifty-year-old drunk drug addicts still runnin' 'round talkin' 'bout they 'dis and 'dat. We know when to quit. And, it's quittin' time for me. I'm clocking out.

Bobby:

Where you gon' go?!

Steve:

Cali.

Bobby:

What the fuck is a Cali?!

Steve:

Look at a goddamn map sometime, shit! It's in Colombia.

Bobby:

(staring at Steve quizzically) Let me get this straight, you call yourself retiring from The Life by running to the literal cocaine capital of the world?!

You thank you slick? You ain't retiring, nigga; you promoting yaself.

Steve:

I'm just a black man going to Colombia to caveman me a chica, drag her back to my cave, and put babies in her.

Bobby:

What if she get all fat and shit?

Steve:

I'ma eat everything she cook and get fat right wit' her big ass!

They both laugh.

Bobby:

Do you understand Spanish?

Steve:

(looking at Bobby unbelievingly) You don't?! Bobby, we was born and raised around these people. How you don't know Spanish?!

Bobby:

I don't know. I didn't understand it, so I didn't listen to the shit.

Steve:

Idioto!

Bobby:

Now, I know that.

Steve:

I'm just the opposite. I need to know everything I don't know. Especially a language being spoken around me that's constantly being used by my friends and enemies. I still speak it broke up sometimes, right, but I understand the shit out of it.

Bobby:

Well, I guess that's it, then. When you pulling up?

Steve:

Probably March or April.

Bobby:

I'm gon' miss you, dog.

Steve:

Right back atcha.


Scene 6-Cali, Colombia. April 17, 2008.

Steve walks down a main street in Cali that's no different from the streets he grew up in. He's drawing attention from everyone, being the only black American man in Cali, looking like a tourist. All of the men ask him if he's looking for drugs, or women, or both, while all of the prostitutes grin and rub him, offering themselves.

As he enters a club of some sort, a group of four men watch him closely.

In the club, ladies of all shapes and sizes strut around topless with dollar bills stuffed into their respective thongs. As individual women approach Steve, he politely nods them away and takes a seat at the bar.

Bartender:

What'll it be?

Steve:

A beer and a tequila.

The DJ's voice booms from the speakers.

DJ:

Please welcome a house favorite to the stage…SONRISAAAAAAAAA!!!!!

Steve takes a deep breath and exhales heavily as the most beautiful woman he's ever seen saunters onto the stage, black hair pulled tight into a ponytail with a blue flower on the right side of her scalp. She dons a black trench coat and blue high-heels.

Prophex-La Medicina booms from the speakers as Sonrisa begins her routine. The opening credits roll to her dancing to this song, with the occasional shot of Steve staring at her.

INTRO ENDS

# Part 1:
# The Good

ACT 2: SCENE 7

Sonrisa removes her coat, revealing the body of an angel covered in a white two-piece bikini. She locks eyes with Steve and is momentarily shocked to a halt as her heart skips a beat.

Steve takes a deep breath as his heart jumps when he catches Sonrisa's stare. Sonrisa never looks anywhere else as she unconsciously dances more seductively, inadvertently sending Steve a message with her body.

This works, because Steve reaches into his pocket, extracting a 100-dollar bill. He approaches the stage. Sonrisa gyrates toward him, bends down slowly, reaches for the bill, and, as their hands touch, special effects shows sparks starting at their fingertips, shooting through their arms and hitting their hearts, causing them to beat faster. They both physically react to this sensation, never losing eye contact, until Sonrisa, slightly flushed, turns, reaches behind her back, pulls the string on her bikini top, takes a few steps, faces the crowd, and slowly exposes her perfect breasts.

A topless waitress walks up to Steve, pokes his shoulder, and thrusts a tray toward him that holds his beer and tequila shot. He downs the shot and grabs the beer, tossing a 20-dollar bill onto the tray, nodding to the waitress, saying in Spanish…

Steve:

Keep the change.

Sonrisa's song and dance come to an end. She leaves the stage slowly, looking at Steve as she does.

At the bar, Steve sits and orders another beer and tequila shot, and he starts questioning the bartender, Freddie.

Steve:

Hey, Sonrisa, is that her stage name or her real name?

Freddie:

Both. You here for business or pleasure? And, for both, I mean cocaine.

Steve laughs, causing Freddie to grin.

Steve:

Naw, I'm a resident now.

Freddie:

Why here?

Steve:

Why not? It's as good a place as any to do nothing. Nice weather, nicer women.

A pretty little waitress walks up, places an order with Freddie, and grins at Steve, rubbing his knee, saying…

Waitress:

Maybe later, hch?

Steve:

Maybe.

Steve thinks to himself that she looks to be around fifteen or sixteen years old. Freddie returns, placing four bottles of beer and eight shots on the young waitress's tray. She then disappears into the tables.

Steve downs his shot.

Meanwhile: Backstage, Sonrisa stares into a mirror, grinning slightly as topless strippers all clamor around, reaching for makeup and talking wildly. She twirls her crucifix, thinking about the black tourist she just saw.

Meanwhile: At the bar, Steve finishes off his beer when Sonrisa takes him by surprise as she sits next to him. He turns to face her, and she follows suit with a smile on her face. They both extend their right hands toward one another and shake, never losing eye contact.

Special effects show not only sparks in their arms but a visual of their hearts' main valves stretching toward one another, connecting, and their heartbeats bang loudly as they synchronize, causing both of them to hold their chests momentarily.

Freddie speaks, bringing them back to the real world.

Freddie:

Can I get you two anything? A drink, a room?

All three laugh.

Steve:

I'm Steve.

Sonrisa:

Sonrisa.

They both smile at each other.

Sonrisa:

Bye, Freddie.

Steve:

Yeah, adios, Freddie.

Freddie nods.

Freddie:

You two have fun.

Luck Mervil-Mezanmi plays throughout the scene as outside Steve studies his surroundings, while Sonrisa wears the look of a nervous schoolgirl who's walking home with a boy she has a crush on.

Steve:

I've never seen a prostitute look nervous before.

Sonrisa:

I'm not a prostitute…anymore.

Steve:

I'm sorry I assumed that. It looks as if congratulations are in order; you said you're not a prostitute anymore.

Sonrisa:

It's a long story.

Steve:

I'd like to hear it whenever you have the time. If you don't have your way with me tonight, then kick me out in the morning.

He smiles at her as she laughs.

Steve:

I feel a helluva lot better knowing that you aren't a prostitute.

Sonrisa:

Why's that?

Steve:

Gives me hope that a lady as beautiful as you can possibly become mine.

She smiles bashfully, looking at the ground.

Sonrisa:

So, where are you from in the U.S.?

Steve:

Chicago, Illinois.

Sonrisa:

(in an excited voice) Chicago, huh? I've heard many things.

Steve:

As I have about Colombia.

She fiddles with the crucifix around her neck.

Sonrisa:

Why'd you follow me out of the club?

Steve:

That look in your eyes wasn't an invitation?

She blushes, he smiles.

Steve:

How'd you know that I'd follow you?

Sonrisa:

Because men will follow pretty girls anywhere.

Steve:

Touché.

Sonrisa:

No, I'm asking for a reason. I need to know if—

Steve:

—If my temperature rose to 100 degrees when we made eye contact, or if I couldn't tell whether my heart was going to explode or stop altogether when we shook hands? Or, better yet, if I'm doing everything in my power not take you right here in the middle of the street, in front of all of these donkeys and people and just have my way with you? Was that it?

Sonrisa:

(exhaling deeply while turning red) Exactly.

Steve:

Not to mention the fact that I thought I'd lose you forever if I let you go through that door without me.

Her eyes widen as she stares at him, smiling widely, causing him to smile.

Steve:

They named you right, Sonrisa. It's contagious.

Sonrisa:

Gracias.

Steve stops abruptly, listening.

Steve:

I hate to ruin such a beautiful mood, and I don't know how well you may or may not know the men who are about to try to rob us, but...

He pulls a 9mm from his spine.

Steve:

...it looks as if I'm about to be forced to protect us.

Sonrisa:

What makes you say that?

Steve:

A lone black American stranger in a violent foreign land. (He looks at Sonrisa, grinning devilishly.) Call it a hunch.

He winks at her, and she giggles nervously.

Steve:

You can get closer if you want to, hold my arm?

Sonrisa:

(in Espanol) You're the devil.

He smiles.

Steve:

Can't blame me for trying to get you to hold me. Any reason'll work for me.

They smile at each other as a car pulls up behind them on their left, honking the horn. Upon turning, they see a 2008 black-on-white 500 Mercedes Benz, all windows tinted. As the window rolls down, Steve puts his gun back down his spine. The passenger calls to Sonrisa.

Passenger:

Sonrisa, you-know-who would like to speak to your American friend.

Steve:

You can talk to me directly, friend.

Passenger:

No offense, but I know the lady.

Steve:

Of course you do.

Sonrisa interlocks her right fingers into his left fingers, and the back door opens slightly. Sonrisa guides Steve toward the car.

Sonrisa:

Let's get this over with.

Act 3-Scene 8: An iron gate swings open, exposing a gorgeous mansion with a fountain in the middle of an enormous yard.

Don Jefe, a.k.a. Vibora, looks at the car pulling in and smiles as he sits in a leather chair with his penis currently being sucked by some anonymous lady.

Vibora:

Get out, bitch, hurry, hurry!

In the car, Steve looks at Sonrisa with concern as he notices the contemptuous look in her eyes as they fill with tears.

Steve:

What's wrong, Sunny, are you okay?

She grips his hand tighter and a smile cracks her frown.

Sonrisa:

I'll tell you later, papito.

He squeezes her hand and a tear falls down her cheek. He wipes it away, hooks a finger under her chin, and slowly turns her face toward his.

Steve:

It'll be fine; I'm with you.

The car grinds to a halt, and all five occupants exit, as Vibora and his two most trusted bodyguards look down at them from the giant window in his office. Carlos and Renaldo are their names.

Renaldo:

Boss, what do you think he wants?

Vibora:

The only things one comes to Colombia to get. A pretty woman. He wasted no time in getting one of those, even though she's been a whore her entire life. And cocaine.

Carlos:

He's been telling everybody he's not here for that.

Vibora:

That's what he's supposed to tell everyone. He's a stranger here. What would you say?

The three amigos turn around as Steve, Sonrisa, and the three gentlemen who escorted them here enter the room. Vibora turns on the charm, vibrantly, as Sonrisa stares blankly at her former captor, who greets her first by kissing her cheek, causing her to cringe.

Vibora:

Pretty one, hello, my love, how are you?

Sonrisa:

Fine, Don Jefe.

Vibora:

Aren't you going to introduce us to your American friend?

One of the three escorts tells Vibora...

Male #1:

The nigger has a gun, boss.

Steve:

First of all, my name is not nigger, it's Steve. My friends call me Steve. Second, I do have a gun, but you all sought me out and brought me here. I'm a stranger here in Colombia. Who am I here to hurt?

Vibora:

You speak Spanish? Very good, very good, I'm impressed! You've made your point about the weapon. Keep it. Drink with me, Steve. Would you like a Cuban?

Steve:

A Cuban, why? I got a Colombiana. (winking at a blushing Sonrisa, who smiles at him) Yes, I'll smoke a cigar with you, hermano.

Vibora:

(smiling) Hermano, I like it.

Renaldo holds the box of cigars out to Steve, who takes one. Vibora pours shots of gin into shot glasses and Carlos takes two of them, handing one to Steve, the other to Sonrisa. Once everyone has a drink in their hand, Vibora raises his glass, proposing a toast.

Vibora:

To our new American friend, Steve!

Everyone drinks.

Steve:

Thank you.

Sonrisa:

Just wait a minute.

Vibora:

So, how many kilos of pure do you want?

Steve:

None. I know this surprises everyone, but I can't be the only American who's ever come to Colombia and didn't want drugs.

Vibora:

(looking at all of his employees) The first one we've met in years. I know you didn't come all the way to Colombia, from the Great United States, just to try to turn a whore into a housewife.

Vibora and his henchmen are the only ones laughing when Sonrisa jumps from her seat, screaming at him.

Sonrisa:

I never chose to be a whore, you fucking faggot!!!

Vibora looks at her as if she's lost her mind as one of his men walks toward her briskly. She stands her ground as Steve runs in front of her, guarding her from the approaching male.

Vibora:

Calm down, Chico, calm down. We all know, from years of experience, just what Sonrisa's mouth can do.

His eyes narrow as he stares at her while his men laugh.

Vibora:

Steve, seeing just how brave you are, and how protective you are of the pretty one here, now, I have a reason to ask you to surrender your weapon.

Steve stares defiantly as he reaches for his weapon, causing the men to brace themselves. He hands Chico his gun and goes back to his seat, which calms everyone.

Vibora:

Can I ask you a question?

Steve:

Why not?

Vibora:

You just met Sonrisa today, no?

Steve:

Yes.

Vibora:

How come you're so protective of her?

Steve:

I can't explain it. (He looks at her and she stares right back into his eyes.) But I've never felt this way about any woman before. Yet I feel compelled to protect this one.

Sonrisa is unaware that she now fiddles with her crucifix and remembers the prayer that she's been praying ever since her fifteenth birthday.

Sonrisa's Voiceover:

Please, God, help me. Send me someone to rescue me from this hell that I was born into, please? I don't deserve this. What did I do to deserve this?

Their hearts beat in unison, loudly, as the sound of bass becomes audible as they both touch their hearts.

Heartbeats:

BOOM BOOM, BOOM BOOM!!!

Steve talks to Vibora, while still looking at Sonrisa, never losing eye contact with her.

Steve:

I know a lot of you macho Latinos only truly appreciate the women in your immediate families, so what I'm explaining to you now may be hard, or even impossible, for you to comprehend, but I humbly request that you all stop disrespecting Sonrisa in my presence. Think of me as her personal pit bull. I will do everything in my power to protect her. With or without a gun.

Vibora:

Chico, give Steve his gun back. I can't help but respect a man as brave as this.

Chico hands Steve his pistol.

Vibora:

Tell me, Steve, have you two shared a kiss yet?

Steve:

No.

Vibora:

Yet you are willing to put your life on the line for her?

Steve:

Yes.

Vibora:

Why?!

Steve:

My heart is telling me that she's my destiny.

He and Sonrisa share a smile as he winks at her. He looks at Vibora as he clips the tip from his cigar, placing it into an ashtray on an end table that's between his and Sonrisa's chairs, lights it, and turns to Vibora.

Steve:

Does that answer your question?

They lock eyes. Vibora senses the triumph in Steve's tone and shifts the conversation to Sonrisa.

Vibora:

So, Pretty One, it seems as if you've found a knight in shining armor.

Sonrisa:

(looking at Vibora with a slight air of confidence) It looks that way.

Vibora:

Well, if Steve here is serious about not wanting any cocaine...? (He looks at Steve for confirmation, and Steve nods in the affirmative. Then, I wish you two the best of luck. (to Chico) Chico, take them back to where you found them.

Steve and Sonrisa rise as Vibora comes from behind his desk, right hand extended toward Steve, who shakes it.

Vibora:

It was nice meeting you, my friend.

Steve:

Back atcha.

Vibora:

(to Sonrisa) Pretty One.

Sonrisa:

Vibora.

Sonrisa turns and exits brusquely.

Steve:

We'll have to do this again sometime.

Vibora:

I have a feeling we will.

Outside, Sonrisa cries on the porch when Steve runs to her, turning her towards himself, lifting her face up, drying her tears.

Steve:

Mi muneca, what's wrong?

Sonrisa:

I hate him so much.

Upstairs, Vibora, Renaldo, Carlos, and the other nameless henchmen watch Chico and the original Passenger as they watch Sonrisa cry into Steve's chest.

Vibora:

I don't know what it is about the Pretty One now, but she is crying her eyes out. I've taken her virginity, had her every way she can be had, and yet she looks more beautiful now than she ever has.

On the porch, Steve tells her…

Steve:

Mi amor. (My love.)

Arcangel-Hace Mucho Tiempo plays as she stares into Steve's eyes, caught off guard as he kisses her. She puts her arms around his neck and stands on the tips of her toes as they open their mouths and gently slide their tongues into each other's mouths. Steve squeezes her buttocks, causing her to moan.

Special effects show their internal organs. Their hearts are made of fire, and when they beat the flames engulf their insides, consuming them totally. They share three final pecks, then separate, staring into each other's eyes.

Sonrisa:

Oh, my God, you took my breath away.

Steve:

You started it.

Vibora's eyes literally turn green as he watches the Mercedes get smaller.

Scene 9-9:23 P.M.: Sonrisa opens the door to her house, revealing a small, yet clean abode. Upon entry, she is greeted happily by a fourteen-year-old girl, Anita; a ten-year-old boy, Miguel; and a two-year-old boy named Marcos.

She lifts Marcos and kisses him a few times, giving Anita and Miguel one-armed hugs.

Sonrisas

My babies, how was your day?

Anita and Miguel both moan, exasperated.

Miguel:

Mama, I hate school.

Anita:

I'd hate it, too, if I was stupid.

Miguel:

Shut up, whore.

Sonrisa looks at him, appalled, as he laughs at this statement.

Anita:

Come over here and call me that, idiot!

Sonrisa:

I hate it when you two talk to each other like that. Please stop it. I'm in such a good mood.

Anita:

Why, Mama?

Sonrisa:

I'll girl talk with you about it later, chica.

Anita:

You met a man?!

Sonrisa:

Oh, my God, nina, he's so....

She squeals in delight.

Sonrisa:

He's so everything!

Miguel:

( running up to his mother and sister, chanting) Mama has a boyfriend,

Mama has a boyfriend. (He giggles as he sits in Sonrisa's lap, tickling his baby brother and sticking his finger inches away from his sister's face.)

Sonrisa:

Be nice, Miggy. (to Anita) Did you feed them?

Anita:

(sighing) Yes, Mama, I fed your ninos. I ate, too, if you care.

Sonrisa playfully pushes Anita's face.

Sonrisa:

Of course I care, mami. (She repeatedly, loudly kisses her cheek as she squirms away, laughing. She says to the boys) Okay, time to get ready for bed.

Miguel pouts and makes a noise.

Miguel:

You only want us to go to bed so you can tell Nita about your boyfriend.

Sonrisa:

(teasingly) You know you and Marcos are my two favorite men, papi. (She kisses Marcos on the cheek and puts him down. He follows his brother.)

Anita:

Mama, you know I don't like when you bring men over.

Sonrisa:

It's different this time, I swear.

Anita lies down, placing her head in Sonrisa's lap, allowing her to stroke her hair as they talk.

Sonrisa:

I was onstage and, about a minute into my dance, I caught the eyes of a black American tourist. And, Nita, I've never felt my heart pound like it did tonight. And when we touched...oh, my God, mi amiga, I shivered all over. (Anita laughs.) This must be what I missed out on when I was your age, because I've never had a real boyfriend. Anyway, when we finally introduced ourselves to each other and shook hands, I thought my heart would explode out of my chest. We were walking down the street, and he was so charming, funny, and cute. Then Vibora's men drove up and would've ruined the moment, but I reached out and held Steve's hand, we tightened our grips, and all of my anxieties went away. Once we got to Vibora's house, I was on the verge of crying. Steve noticed this and said, "Sunny." (She squeals.) He called me Sunny. He said, "Sunny, what's wrong, are you okay?" I told him I'd tell him later. He squeezed my hand and said, "It'll be fine; I'm with you." (Anita smiles and coos with envy.) Then, when Vibora started to talk down to me (emotes like she did in Vibora's office), I called him a fucking faggot! Chico charged me like he was going to hit me, and Steve rushed in front of me, guarding me. When Vibora asked him why he would possibly risk his life for a woman he just met, he just stared at me and told him, "Because my heart tells me to; she's my destiny."

Anita rises up and looks at her mother with eyes filled with awe.

Anita:

Sounds like something from a romance novel or a movie.

Sonrisa:

But it's not, mi amor, it's real life, and it's happening to me. And, I still haven't told you the best part yet. When I stormed out, crying on the stairs, Steve came to me on the porch, wiped away my tears, calling me his baby doll, and kissed me. Oh, my God, that kiss, Nita! Set me on fire.

They giggle loudly as they touch foreheads.

Sonrisa:

And, he's taking me out tomorrow.

Anita:

Mama, you look and sound so happy. I've never seen you this happy before, ever.

Sonrisa:

I've never felt like this before, because nothing ever made me feel like this. I'm about to be thirty, and I've never had a boyfriend or been in love.

Tears begin to fall and Anita pulls her mother to her bosom, rocking her as she strokes her hair.

Anita:

Oh, Mama, it's okay, mi amor, it's okay. It's finally your turn to experience true love and happiness, mamita.

Sonrisa:

(rubbing her crucifix) I truly do think he's the one that I've been praying for, chiquita. You should've seen the look in his eyes when Chico approached me. There was fire in them, the passion in his voice. He was truly ready to fight and die for me. And we just met today.

Anita:

(voice straining slightly) Mamita, you don't think he's like the others…

Sonrisa:

(rising, placing Anita's head onto her bosom) No, no, no, no, nina, I can feel it in my bones. Those two were animals, Nita, monsters. I should've never let them anywhere near you. Steve's different, I swear to you.

Anita:

You'll forgive me if it takes me a while to warm up to him?

Sonrisa:

Yes. I only ask that you give him this one chance. You didn't see me look this way because of any other man, not even Marcos' father. Nina, he's different. Trust me.

They enjoy a few seconds of silence when Miguel and Marcos run in jumping on the couch in only pajama bottoms.

Miguel:

Why are you crying, Mama? I heard you.

Sonrisa:

Because I'm happy.

Miguel:

Aye!!! You women, you cry when you're happy, cry when you're sad, cry when you're mad. Make up your minds already.

He sticks his tongue out at Anita, rubbing his eyes, mimicking crying, as Sonrisa feigns being hurt, reaches out, and tickles him.

Sonrisa:

So mean to us women, papito.

Anita:

(grabbing his forearm) Shut up, stupid!

Miguel:

(through laughter) Idiota, let me go!

Sonrisa:

(kissing Marcos) Your brother is so mean.

They all gang up on a giggling and squirming Miguel.

Act 3-Scene 10-11:15 A.M. The Next Day.

Chino and Nacho-Bebe Bonita plays as Steve stands in front of Sonrisa's club in a blue suit, watching her approach. She wears an all-white, silk spaghetti-strapped dress, with no bra, and white high-heels, with her hair pulled back in a tight ponytail, with a white shawl over her shoulders. Steve has a single rose in one hand, and a beats-by-dre speaker with an iPod inserted into it.

They smile at each other as they hug.

Steve:

You look beautiful. (He hands her the rose.) Very elegant.

Sonrisa:

(smile beaming) Thank you, mi amor. You look dashing, very suave.

She snaps the stem from the rose, fixes it onto the right side of her hair, and strikes a pose for Steve, showing off.

Sonrisa:

(smiling) You like?

Steve:

Most definitely.

She walks up to him and they share a quick peck…

Sonrisa:

Shall we?

Steve:

Lead the way.

Steve places the speaker into his inside jacket pocket.

Sonrisa:

What's with the speaker?

Steve:

It's a surprise.

Sonrisa:

I like surprises.

Steve:

(grinning at her) I'll bet.

They lock arms and start their short walk to a restaurant.

Steve:

Your English is very good.

Sonrisa:

Thank you. A lot of Americans come through Colombia. Your Spanish isn't too bad.

Steve:

I grew up in a Latino neighborhood. That's why I had no aversions to coming to a Latin country.

Sonrisa:

I want to know everything there is to know about you.

Steve:

I'm a simple man; there isn't much to tell.

Sonrisa:

(holding him back and turning his face toward hers, staring deeply into his eyes) I look into your eyes and see so many emotions, so much pain and yet your heart is so big. You're an enigma. I can feel it in my soul that there is so much more to you that either you know or just don't let out intentionally. But, whatever it is, I intend to figure it out. You're special. I've never met a man who would do what you did for me last night, especially when we just met. And the things you said, why did you say those things?

Steve:

Because I meant them.

Sonrisa:

Why, papi, why did you mean them? What compelled you?

Steve:

You.

Sonrisa touches her cross.

Sonrisa:

What about me?

Steve:

I can't explain it, but when I first laid eyes on you, it felt like a hammer dropped on my heart. And when Chico ran up on you, I didn't even realize that I was moving, or how fast. All I knew was that I'd be damned if I let any one of those animals lay a finger on you.

Eli-Tu Me Haces Volar plays as Sonrisa throws herself into his arms and slides her tongue into his mouth. She stands on the tips of her toes as he squeezes her buttocks.

Sonrisa backs away with tears streaking her cheeks. Steve wipes them away.

Sonrisa:

I can't explain why I feel like this or why you bring all of these tears and emotions out of me, but the things you say don't surprise me, and they should.

Steve:

You've been holding back for so long, it's time for you to let go. Would you do for me what I did for you yesterday?

Sonrisa:

Si, mi amor. Si.

Steve:

Do you think that there's anything that I can tell you about me that would make you stop feeling the way you feel?

Sonrisa:

No, querido. Do you?

Steve:

Not at all.

Sonrisa:

Do you believe in love at first sight?

Steve:

I didn't, until I saw you.

Sonrisa:

It was like a magnet.

They stare into each other's eyes momentarily. She stands on the tips of her toes and pecks his lips.

Sonrisa:

And you said there wasn't much to you. Let's go eat.

Meanwhile: Chico, his usual passenger, Javier; and their backseat goon, Tomas, watch Steve and Sonrisa through the tinted windows of the Benz.

Chico:

Damn, that whore looks good.

Javier:

She's happy for once in her life.

Tomas:

She is beaming.

In the restaurant, Steve and Sonrisa sit in a corner booth.

Sonrisa:

So, tell me about your childhood.

Steve:

My grandmother raised me, along with the streets. Mainly the streets. Never knew my father, barely knew my mother. When I was around seven or eight, she left and never came back. I think she was on drugs. I'd rather believe she was addicted to something than to believe she left because she couldn't stand her kid. At about nine or ten, I took to the streets, started selling drugs and running into drug houses, robbing them. Sometimes killing them. Eighteen or nineteen, I got tired of doing that, but it was also all that I knew, so...you know the rest. Luckily, I was always a person who thought ahead, so I used to take some of the money and put it in a bank account I started. I did one year in prison after getting caught with a gun. I read my time away. And, now, I'm here with you.

Sonrisa:

Did you ever kill any kids?

Steve:

Hell no. We were crooks, not animals. It was bad enough we were making them orphans; we'd never make them corpses.

Sonrisa:

Do you have any children?

Steve:

No. The one I almost had, she had a miscarriage.

Sonrisa:

How did that make you feel?

Steve:

I felt a lot of things. Happy at first, I think by me not knowing my father. I'd've tried that much harder to be a good one. Disappointed when she lost it. I felt relieved, not because she lost it but at the realization that at that time in my life it may not have been the best thing for a child. Do you think any less of me, knowing all of this?

· Sonrisa:

Never, if anything it makes me feel that much closer to you. And, besides, after going through what I've been through, you learn not to judge others. Your past seems tame when measured against mine. I'm hoping you don't think any less of me when I tell you what I've been through.

Steve reaches across the table, grabs her hand, and stares directly into her eyes.

Steve:

I assure you, you don't have to worry about me leaving you. I'm in it now. So, get that out of your mind.

Sonrisa smiles and catches a tear before it falls.

Sonrisa:

Before my mother died, she told me that on the day I was born Vibora gunned my father and uncles down after they stole drugs and money from his father. Having no other family, he forced my mother to work as a prostitute in that very same house we went to yesterday. When I first bled, at twelve, he took my virginity, then, the very next day, forced me into prostitution. My mother blew her brains out on my fifteenth birthday. So, instead of a Quinceañera, I was forced to entertain four men at once and plan my mother's funeral right after she committed suicide. When I turned twenty-one, Vibora, in what's mercy for him, released me from that prison, but, like you and what you did, prostitution was all that I knew. Three years ago I met a man, thought that he loved me, and I him, until I told him this story and woke up the next morning to an empty bed and his son in my belly. My baby, Marcos, is two now.

Steve:

Is he your only child?

Sonrisa:

The only one that I gave birth to.

Steve:

How many do you have? And, tell me everything.

Sonrisa:

Three. Anita is fourteen. (visualizing) About a week after I left Vibora's bordello, I found Anita, six at the time, filthy and eating out of the trash. I approached her, she told me that she didn't have any family. I knocked on a few doors, no one claimed her, so I did. In the time she's been with me, two men have forced themselves on her. That's when I quit selling my body. I'd never forgive myself if I kept placing her in harm's way. Two years after finding her, we found Miguel, four then, ten now, sleeping in an abandoned car.

Steve:

Sonrisa, you're a beautiful woman.

Sonrisa:

(smiling) Thank you, papi.

Steve:

After everything you've been through, still beautiful, still finding time to try to save us lost mortals and give orphans a better life.

Sonrisa:

(smiling) I don't want any children going through what we've been through.

Steve:

Same thing I used to think before the miscarriage. Funny thing, that young lady and I broke up after that.

Their food arrives.

Steve:

I know I told you to leave your money at home, but I forgot my wallet. You did bring some money, didn't you?

Sonrisa gasps in mock as Steve grins at her.

Sonrisa:

El Diablo!

They share a laugh and let their waiter know that they are fine, but Steve motions for the waiter to leave the bottle of red wine that he just filled their glasses from, saying…

Steve:

(looking at Sonrisa, yet talking to the waiter) I'm trying to help her get out of that beautiful dress as much as possible.

All three laugh.

Sonrisa:

(grinning at Steve) Diablo!

Steve grins and winks at her as she blushes.

Montage footage rolls, showing them enjoying their meal, laughing. Sonrisa laughs at Steve as he fans his mouth after ingesting a spicy yellow pepper. He holds up another and acts as if he'll feed it to her. She backs away, smiling the entire time as Steve dabs sweat from his forehead.

The in-house mariachi band finishes playing a song for them and they applaud. Steve holds up the bowl with the yellow peppers, offering them to the band, who all laugh as Steve tips them, handsomely, according to the reaction of the lead singer, after he unfolds the American $50. The singer happily turns to the band, signaling, and they strike up another song, causing the patrons to applaud. Sonrisa stares adoringly at Steve, who just smiles and shrugs his shoulders.

It's now 7:30 P.M. when Steve notices that it's now dark outside. He stands, extending his right hand to Sonrisa, who accepts. He walks her to the center of the dance floor and lets her stand there, alone, briefly, as he runs to the jukebox, inserts two coins, and walks briskly back to Sonrisa, who quickly wraps her arms around his neck.

Steve:

See how I made everyone in the restaurant stare at my date?

Sonrisa smiles.

Steve:

I know you didn't think I'd let you leave this restaurant without us getting our arms around each other, did you?

Sonrisa:

El Diablo!

He smiles and winks at her as Yandel-En La Oscuridad erupts from the speakers and they sway to the song in its entirety, occasionally breaking away, allowing Sonrisa to twirl.

When the song ends, they sway with Sonrisa's head on Steve's chest for five seconds of silence. The patrons applaud, bringing them back to reality, smiling at one another, sharing a quick kiss.

8 P.M. They walk on a beach, talking, hand in hand.

Sonrisa:

I had a nice time, mi amor, the best day of my life.

Steve:

The night's not over yet.

Sonrisa:

I'm getting cold.

(teasing her) Should've brought a jacket.

Sonrisa:

(playfully swatting his arm) Diablo!

Steve smiles, extracting the speaker from his jacket pocket, placing it on the sand.

Steve:

I got a proposition for you.

Sonrisa:

(shooting him a suspicious glance) What is it?!

Steve:

My blazer, for your dress?

He raises an eyebrow in anticipation of her answer as he walks up to her.

Steve:

So, what's it gon' be?

Sonrisa:

Papi, I'm cold.

Steve:

So, that just means the odds are in my favor.

He walks behind her, putting his arms around her waist, kissing her cheek, then the nape of her neck, causing her to moan in ecstasy as she tilts her head back and he kisses her lips.

He bends his knees slightly, grabbing the hem of her dress, raising it, sliding his fingers into her panties, massaging her clitoris, making her purr and smile, exhaling deeply.

Sonrisa:

Aye, papi, besame. (Kiss me.)

Steve:

(kissing her) I thought you said you were cold, mami. You feel pretty hot to me.

Sonrisa:

You should know, mi amor, you started that fire.

They kiss as she holds his right hand in place.

Sonrisa:

So, you'd make a girl freeze just to get her out of her clothes?

Steve:

You can't blame the Devil for using every weapon at his disposal to get an angel out of her clothes. And, not just any angel, but you.

Sonrisa:

(turning and facing him) My own personal Devil.

They kiss passionately as it becomes her turn to slide her hand down his pants, stroking his erection.

Steve:

Playing with cats just doesn't arouse the woman.

Sonrisa backs away from him, slowly dropping the straps on her dress as Steve turns around.

Steve:

I'm trying to save that image for later.

A few seconds later, her dress falls over his face. He removes his coat and hands it back to her. She takes it and hurriedly wraps it around her body. Steve turns to face her.

Steve:

Now, would you dance for me?

She smiles shyly.

Steve:

What's wrong?

I've always danced as a stripper or prostitute. I've never danced for mi novio (my boyfriend).

Steve:

That means we're both in for a treat.

Sonrisa:

I'll do it. Under one condition.

Steve:

(grinning) El Diabla! What's that?

Sonrisa:

Kiss me.

He approaches her and they hungrily take each other's tongues into their mouths, her stroking his hard penis, him squeezing her buttocks, causing her to stand on the tips of her toes.

She looks up at him with tears in her eyes.

Sonrisa:

My entire life has been spent in sexual slavery. I've never been this wet between the legs. Never felt my heart beat for love. Never opened up sexually. I always closed up, waiting for it to be over.

Steve:

So, emotionally you're still a sexual virgin?

Sonrisa:

Si. Now, go play the music.

Steve walks over to the speaker, presses a button, and Seu Jorge-Tive Razao blares from the speaker. Sonrisa turns her back to Steve, rolls up the sleeves on the blazer, takes a deep breath, exhales slowly, and turns seductively toward him, donning the look of a master temptress, staring brazenly at her prey. She slides her right hand slowly down her cleavage as she starts to sway gently to the music.

Steve nods to the music as Sonrisa grins at him, her movements motivating him, his eyes goading her on. Steve reaches into his pants, adjusting his erection. This makes Sonrisa smile widely.

Sonrisa, overcome with desire and tired of this coquettish game, stops suddenly, placing her hands on her hips in a way that displays her breasts. She bites her bottom lip as she admires the way Steve ogles her flesh.

Sonrisa:

Ven aqui, papi. (Come here, baby.)

Steve obeys.

Upon arrival, they embrace, sharing a kiss. Steve guides her to the sand, where she raises her knees toward her chest, inviting Steve to do whatever he wishes. Sensing this, Steve starts his descent, kissing her cleavage, gently nibbling on each nipple, sliding his tongue into her navel, and, hip finally, taking her clitoris with his tongue.

Her eyes burst open as she audibly gasps, reaching down with both hands to hold his head in place, as orgasm after orgasm shakes her entire body. She moans through her bitten bottom lip, as tears leave her closed eyes, she cries out.

Sonrisa:

Oh, my God, papi, mi amor, don't stop, you're taking my breath away.

After a few more seconds of this, Steve raises up, looking down on his lover, wiping his chin, as he notices Sonrisa, flushed, breathing heavily, says to him…

Sonrisa:

(smiling) I'm sorry, mi amor.

Steve:

You have nothing to apologize for. If you didn't leave something on my chin, that means I was doing it wrong.

She touches his lips.

Sonrisa:

Lay down, mi amor.

He does this, and she slips out of his coat as she takes position on her knees. As soon as Steve is on his back, Sonrisa furiously snatches his pants and underwear to his ankles, freeing his erection. She massages his scrotum and takes him into her mouth. Steve closes his eyes and tries to keep his breathing steady as he looks up at the stars.

Sonrisa rises, pulls her underwear off, throws her leg over Steve's waist while grabbing his piece. Once she has him in her hand, she rises, closing her eyes, placing him inside of her gently, moaning as she dips gracefully onto his midsection, as he assists her by grabbing her buttocks, causing her to purr like the kitten she is.

Their rhythm is in sync, as they accelerate progressively, she moans as she slams down, her juices spilling onto his waistline. She slows, biting her bottom lip and tilting her head back. Steve leans up and they share a deep, tongue-filled kiss. He grabs her shoulder, expertly turning her, laying her on her back, raising his arms behind her knees, thrusting into Sonrisa, who squeezes his behind, encouraging him to move faster, which he does. She sticks her tongue into his ear and bites his ear lobe, causing him to exhale audibly.

Steve:

(gazing into her eyes) You know I bite back, don't you?

Sonrisa:

I dare you to, papi, ravage me!

He goes for her neck, which she freely offers. He licks, kisses, and nibbles her there. He goes for her left ear, licking the inside, then biting down on her earlobe, they share a deep kiss.

Sonrisa:

I've never felt this way in my life, mi amor. Never!

Steve:

Me, either, chiquita. What did you do to me?

She pulls him to her and they briefly exchange tongues.

Steve:

It's a good thing I came here to live.

Sonrisa:

Why?

Steve:

Because I'd've had to abandon my life had I came as a tourist.

Sonrisa:

( exhaling deeply, smiling) Oh, papi.

Her eyes roll to the back of her head as she moans.

Sonrisa:

Oh, my God!

Splashdown! As yet another orgasm rocks her body, she rubs her crucifix, mumbling thanks to her god in Spanish, to herself, as Steve slows his strokes, admiring Sonrisa's body while he holds her hips.

Sonrisa:

Take me from behind, papi.

She bends over and Steve enters her slowly. She bites her bottom lip as he begins to pump. She leans back toward him, opening her mouth for a kiss as he caresses her breasts and she places her hands on his, to keep them in place.

Sonrisa:

I need you to go into my ass, papito.

Steve's eyes widen with delight.

Steve:

Yeah?

Sonrisa;

Every time I've been forced to lay with men, it's been against my will, it's been vile and disgusting. Every time I think about them sickens me, carino. Now that I have you, my first good man, I need you to change all of my bad memories of sex and turn them into something beautiful. Please, mi amor, change my mind?

She opens her mouth and receives his tongue, cradling his head in her left arm.

Steve:

Anything for you, mi amor.

They end their kiss with a soft, yet moist, peck, as Sonrisa leans forward bracing herself, biting her bottom lip, eyes widening in pleasure, and a slight discomfort as Steve penetrates her anus.

Sonrisa:

Start slow, papi.

Steve obeys, not wanting to hurt this woman, only wishing to make her Sonrisa. Coincidentally, that is exactly what Sonrisa's doing at the moment, as she continuously thanks her god while bracing herself with her left hand, holding her cross in her right.

Steve exhales audibly and shakes visibly as he releases his load into Sonrisa's backside. She falls onto her stomach and Steve lies beside her. She immediately snuggles into him and he embraces her, grabbing his coat and covering them both. He then grabs his underwear and pants, pulling them up quickly. They share a few kisses.

Sonrisa:

I feel so good right now, mi amor. I've never, ever felt this way in my life. This must be how teenage girls feel. My nerves are exploding, right now.

Steve:

So, you've never had a boyfriend, not one?

Sonrisa:

Marcos' father, but deep down I knew he wasn't what I was waiting for. And, he didn't even come close to cracking my emotional wall. The first time I laid eyes on you, I felt it start to crumble. It took fifteen years for me to experience this, eighteen if you count when Vibora stole my virginity.

Steve:

How old are you?

Sonrisa:

Twenty-nine. I'll be thirty next month.

Steve:

Me, too.

Sonrisa:

What day?

Steve:

May 13.

Sonrisa sits up, looking at him, wide-eyed and smiling.

Sonrisa:

That's my birthday, too.

They kiss. Sonrisa touches her crucifix.

Steve:

Star-crossed lovers.

Sonrisa:

Two Tauros.

Steve:

I see you touch your cross a lot.

                              Sonrisa:

I just recently started doing that.

                              Steve:

Why's that?

                              Sonrisa:

Trying to figure out if you're the one I've been praying for since my, or should I say, our fifteenth birthday.

                              Steve:

And, what's the verdict?

Their heartbeats BOOM!!! audibly and they both reach out, touching each other's chest.

                              Sonrisa:

What do you think?

She kisses him.

                              Sonrisa:

Do you believe in God?

                              Steve:

No.

Sonrisa:

Why not, mi amor?

Steve:

To make a long story short, it just never stuck to me like it does to others. Deep down I just want to live life. When I think about religion, I don't feel anything there, or anything missing. I don't really care how the world was made; any explanation can't be proven, they're all just theories that people have to blindly believe. I don't knock it, I know some people need something. (looking at Sonrisa, stroking her cheek, she nods into his hand) Lucky for me, I've found what I've been searching for.

She smiles at him, leans in, kissing him.

Steve:

And last, but not least, I'm too much of a realist to just up and believe anything that can't be fully explained or proven. Basically, I've just been trying to do good to those that I feel in my heart need or deserve it. Taking the good with the bad in my own life, not worrying why either is happening. I've wreaked enough havoc, but, even though I knew it was wrong, the people that I robbed and killed were crooks like I was, that's how I slept at night. Now, I'm through killing and robbing people. I have to do something helpful. Something, anything.

Sonrisa just stares at him, admiringly.

Sonrisa:

I told you there was more to you than you wanted to let out.

Steve:

It doesn't bother you that I don't believe in any of that stuff?

Sonrisa:

No. I've been praying and waiting for you for too long just to turn you away now. I can feel it in my heart and soul that you're the one, and, the way I see it, God sent me an atheist savior. And, just out of pure curiosity, I have to keep you around to figure out why. Maybe you're here so that I make a believer out of you; maybe you're here for me to learn that, just because someone doesn't believe in God, doesn't necessarily mean that they're a bad person, or that they can't be used for good. Whatever the reason, or purpose, you're fulfilling one of your duties, now. That's how I know you're a good person, with good in you.

Steve:

What am I doing?

Sonrisa:

You're making me the happiest woman in the world right now, and I've never been happy in my life.

J-Alvarez-Junto Al Amanecer plays as they kiss deeply, and the scene fades into the sun rising, with them sleeping, her head resting on his chest, his left arm around her waist.

As the sun comes into view, Sonrisa stirs as she feels Steve raise up, resting on his elbows. She rolls up, sitting on his left thigh, covering herself with the blazer, looking at her lover, as he stares at the sun. She smiles at him as she uses her left hand to gently turn his face toward hers.

Sonrisa:

Mirame. (Look at me.)

He stares into her eyes, and she smiles.

Sonrisa:

Tocame. (Touch me.)

He takes his right hand and rubs down her chest, middle finger down her cleavage.

Sonrisa:

(more intense) Papi, tocame!

He squeezes her behind, then massages her clitoris, gently sliding his finger inside of her, causing her to moan in ecstasy while biting her bottom lip.

Sonrisa:

Besame.

He obeys, kissing her.

After their brief snuggle, they both look at the sun as it creeps over the water, its beams dancing on the surface, shimmering like Christmas lights.

Sonrisa:

What're you thinking, mi amor?

Steve:

(turning her face to his, then pointing at the sun) That as beautiful as that is, it doesn't compare to this. (He rubs her cheek with his thumb.)

They peck lips.

Sonrisa:

How do you feel about me now?

Steve:

I love you.

She squeals and smiles brightly.

Steve:

I can't explain it, can't explain why or how it happened, but it did. And, you're the first woman I've ever told that to, first. Women usually tell me that first. But, this is what it is. How else can you explain my insides burning when I think of you going back to work in that club, taking your clothes off for a living. I can't have that. In Vibora's office, I felt, and shared your hatred for him, didn't even know why, just did, and do. That's what made do what I did. I feel as if I don't have a choice but to love and protect you.

Sonrisa cries and peppers his face with kisses, saying…

Sonrisa:

Mi amor, mi amor, I love you, too. I love you, so much, mi amor.

Steve:

So, the only thing that's left new, is, what do we do about it?

They share an intimate embrace as the scene fades to black.

Act 4- Scene 11: May 13, 2008, appears on the screen and fades as Don Omar-Hasta Abajo plays throughout the beginning of the scene as Steve draws attention from people on the street, as he carefully reads street signs, wearing the latest Black Jumpman Jordans, black jeans, and a crisp white button-up shirt, carrying two bags.

Meanwhile: In Sonrisa's house, she and Anita both primp themselves in her bedroom mirror with Anita singing along with Don Omar. Miguel plays with Marcos and briefly looks out of the living room window, where he sees six of his female neighbors, flirting with what looks to be the only black American stranger he's expecting, as they rub his arm, while giggling in his face.

Miguel:

(yelling to his mother, while picking up Marcos) Mama, you'd better come rescue your boyfriend before the neighbor girls get him!

Meanwhile: In the bedroom: Sonrisa and Anita both squeal with excitement as they first check themselves, then one another as they rub each other's ponytails back. They both smile widely and giggle loudly.

Sonrisa:

How do I look, chiquita?

Anita:

Beautiful, mamita. And me?

Sonrisa:

Very pretty, nina, very precious.

Outside, Steve advances as best as he can through the swarm of ladies as Sonrisa comes to his rescue, smiling at him, then scowling at her neighbors and lightly swatting them away like the vultures that they are. She gives Steve a hurried peck on the lips, and quickly resumes her reprimanding of the neighbor girls.

Inside the house, Anita holds Marcos as Miguel stands beside her, scowling at Steve as he and Sonrisa enter the room. Steve drops the bags and he embraces Sonrisa, kissing her passionately as Miguel scoffs, causing Anita to lightly punch his upper arm. He swats hers in retaliation as she smiles at them.

Steve:

Happy Birthday.

Sonrisa:

Happy Birthday, carino.

Miguel snipes in Spanish.

Miguel:

I don't like him. He should go back to America!

Anita:

Shut up, Miggy! (running to her mother, shaking Steve's hand) Mama, he's cute.

Steve:

( en Espanol) Thank you for the compliment, Beauty Queen.

Anita gasps in shock and stares at her mother.

Sonrisa:

(grinning, sarcastically teasing her children) Did I forget to mention that he speaks Spanish?

Miguel:

You know you did.

Everyone but Miguel laughs. Steve directs his attention to Anita, while reaching into one of the bags.

Steve:

I have something for you, Nita. (extracting a bouquet of a dozen roses, handing them to her) Hold these for me.

She and Sonrisa both drop their jaws in awe. Steve removes a silver sash that has 'Miss Colombiana' embroidered on it, and places it onto Anita's shoulder, and taps his chin with his finger, as if he's forgetting something. Anita only gawks at her mother, who is looking at her daughter, with playful envy.

Sonrisa:

(pouting teasingly at Steve, who kisses her cheek) But it's my birthday.

Steve:

Calm down, sweetheart. ( He reaches into the bag, removing a black velvet jewelry box.)

Sonrisa and Anita share an audible gasp as the box is opened by Stevie, revealing a shining tiara. Anita squeaks.

Sonrisa:

(watching with watery eyes as Steve places the tiara gently on Anita's head) It's too much, mi amor.

Steve:

Doesn't seem like it's enough for Miss Colombiana, if you ask me. (He grins at Anita.) So, how does it feel to be Miss Colombiana?

A tear makes its way down Anita's cheek, which she quickly wipes away as Sonrisa runs to her side, smiling.

Sonrisa:

I told you he's as charming as the Devil.

Steve:

That's what beauty queens do when the crown is first placed on their heads. So, Anita, you're right on schedule. Can me and Sonrisa be the first to have our pictures taken with Miss Colombiana?

Anita nods, while approaching him, giving him a hug.

Anita:

Gracias, Steve.

Steve:

Think nothing of it.

Miguel:

Girls get everything.

Everyone laughs but Miguel.

Steve:

Patience, Miggy, patience. Come and take this picture with us and Miss Colombiana.

Miguel:

(eyeballing Anita) She wishes she was Miss Colombiana.

Sonrisa:

Be nice, Miggy, it's me and Steve's birthday.

Miguel walks to the group, lifting Marcos as he blends in, standing between Steve and Sonrisa. They smile at each other as Steve holds his phone out and readies them.

Steve:

Smile.

They all pose as Steve takes two quick pictures.

Steve:

I also have something for Marcos.

Miguel:

(snidely) Of course you do.

Sonrisa softly pushes his head as he puts his baby brother down and walks back to the kitchen table. Steve winks and grins back at the ladies, who grin back at him as Sonrisa pulls Anita closer to her side. They watch as Steve removes a brand-new Soccer ball from one of his bags and rolls it to Marcos, who kicks it, to the enjoyment of all, as Steve, Sonrisa, and Anita yell...

GOOOOOOAAAAAAALLLLLL!!!!

Marcos laughs as he chases down his new toy. Steve reaches down into the bag, but is interrupted by Marcos, who approaches him with the ball in hand. Steve picks him up.

Steve:

You like your new ball?!

Sonrisa and Anita wear permanent smiles.

Steve:

(looking at Sonrisa and Anita) Babies are easy to shop for. Watch this. (He picks up at Marcos, bouncing him.) You want to play with your sister's hair? (He leans Marcos toward Anita. Marcos drops the ball and reaches for his sister's hair.)

Sonrisa and Anita laugh as Anita reaches for her tiara. Steve smiles as he puts Marcos down, saying to him...

Steve:

Go show your brother your new ball.

He starts digging around in the bags with both hands, pulling out three iPad boxes.

Steve:

(to Anita) One for you. (to Sonrisa) the birthday girl.

Sonrisa:

Gracias, mi amor.

Anita:

Gracias, Steve.

Steve:

De nada, de nada.

Miguel gets wide-eyed with anticipation.

Steve:

(teasing him) What? This is for me?

Miguel huffs and puffs, folding his arms, to the amusement of everyone that isn't him.

Steve:

Still want me to go back to America?

The ladies look at him. He stays silent as Steve makes his way to him, sitting across from him at the table.

Steve:

Listen to me, Miguel. Your mother has told me everything ( looking back at Anita), and I do mean everything. I'm not leaving. I truly love your mother. I'm here to stay. And, I'm not trying to take you out of the throne as man of the house. But, I am here to help. (He leans in to whisper.) Plus, I can help take some of the pressure off of you, dealing with these two chicas.

Miguel laughs.

Steve:

(extending his right hand for a handshake) Deal?

Miguel:

(smiling) Deal.

They shake hands and Anita leans into her mother's embrace as they wipe tears from their cheeks.

Anita:

Mamita, he's so sweet.

Sonrisa:

I told you he was different, chica. It's the first time that I've ever felt it inside of me. I'm in love.

Anita:

If he can make you this happy, how can I not give him a chance?

Sonrisa:

Gracias, babygirl.

Steve turns and makes his way toward Sonrisa, reaching into his back pocket, extracting an envelope that is filled with something.

Steve:

If only I had something else for the birthday girl.

He waves the envelope in the air, teasing her. Sonrisa gasps.

Sonrisa:

Mi amor, you've already done too much, papi.

Steve:

That's funny, because I was just thinking that I haven't done enough.

She wraps her arms around his neck and they kiss. She grabs the envelope and scurries off, saying...

Sonrisa:

I have something for you.

Steve and Marcos kick the ball to each other while Anita goes to the table and joins Miguel as they both play with their iPads.

Sonrisa comes back into the room, concealing something behind her back.

Sonrisa:

Happy Birthday, mi amor.

Steve:

Baby, thank you, you shouldn't have.

She dangles a silver crucifix, identical to the one she wears.

Sonrisa:

I know you don't believe in—

Steve:

Put it on me. I love it.

She beams and hits him with a barrage of kisses. He lowers his head and she puts the chain on him. He touches her crucifix.

Sonrisa:

It was my mother's. I finally have a birthday that's actually happy.

Steve:

And many more. (He raises his hand, displaying a blue velvet jewelry box. Sonrisa gasps.) Hope you like these.

She opens it, crying, and calls Anita.

Sonrisa:

Nita, look at what Steve gave me.

Two giant diamond earrings glare up at them. Anita touches one, exclaiming...

Anita:

Try them on, mamita!

Sonrisa:

Not now, these are for special occasions only. They're too beautiful, too expensive. (She looks at Steve, who wipes her tears away.) They're too much, mi amor.

Steve:

Out of everything you've been through, it's long overdue for you and your kids to start experiencing the finer things life has to offer.

Sonrisa kisses him. Anita just looks at them with admiration in her eyes, happy that her mother has finally found a decent man.

There's a knock at the door, and many female voices can be heard, telling Sonrisa to open up.

Miguel:

Run, Steve, run. They're going to get you.

Anita, Miguel, and Steve laugh as Sonrisa mumbles curses about the female jackals outside her door, as she goes to open it.

Outside, the eight ladies are, Rosalia, Ilanny, Carmen, Bethany, Helena, Sara, Talia, and Penelope.

Sonrisa:

(closing the door behind her) Mis amigas, go away, you're scaring mi novio (my boyfriend). You already mauled him on his way in.

Helena:

Ladies, check out Sonrisa, she has an American, now she's too good for us.

Rosalita:

She bragged and bragged about him (mocking Sonrisa) 'Oh, chicas, he's so cute and so funny and so sweet, he takes my breath away when he kisses me, I never had so many orgasms in my life.' AYE!!!

Carmen:

And, now she won't let us meet him.

Ilanny:

( pushing up her breasts and adjusting her shirt) She's scared one of us will take him away, no?!

All of the ladies agree, as Sonrisa gets playfully agitated and points at all of her friends.

Sonrisa:

(feigning severity) Malditas, stay away from my boyfriend!

Bethany:

I want to see him…naked.

Sonrisa puts her head into her hands as the brood of ladies laugh in agreement.

Sonrisa:

It's our birthdays, and, I just wanted to spend it with him, plus, it's his first time meeting my babies.

Sarah:

It's his birthday, too?!

Sonrisa:

Si, si.

Talia:

( holding up two tequila bottles) That's why we came, chica.

Penelope:

I know he has a big dick. Not only is she overprotective, she's ditching us. (She holds her hands close together.) Tell me when to stop.

Sonrisa blushes as Penelope slowly separates them, to the other ladies' enjoyment, when Penelope gets impossibly far apart, the ladies get loud in amazement as Sonrisa smiles. Sonrisa grabs a bottle of tequila from Talia.

Sonrisa:

It is our birthday.

Bethany:

That's gonna cost you, chica.

Rosalita:

Just leave the blinds open so we can see it before he puts it in.

They all laugh.

On the other side of the door, Steve, Anita, and Miguel listen.

Outside, Sonrisa tells her friends…

Sonrisa:

I'll let you meet him tomorrow, go, go.

The ladies reluctantly disperse. Sonrisa opens the door and says nothing as she notices the eavesdroppers going in the opposite direction, a little close to the door to not have been listening.

Steve:

I see they gave you a birthday gift.

Sonrisa:

We usually spend our birthdays together, but, things change.

She smiles at him.

Sonrisa:

Plus, I wanted you and me to spend our birthday together, just the two of us, with you getting to know the kids.

Steve:

(He reaches out for her to come to him, and she obliges.) What a coincidence, that's exactly how I wanted to spend today, too.

They kiss. Anita smiles at them. Miguel looks up from his iPad.

Miguel:

Take it to the bedroom, already.

Anita waves her hand at him in admonishment.

Steve:

Happy Birthday, sweetheart.

Sonrisa:

Happy Birthday, mi amor.

There's a knock at the door. Sonrisa sighs heavily, causing Anita to answer it. A pizza delivery boy holds two boxes and a bag. Steve pulls out a wad of money, peels off two bills, and hands it to Anita. Miguel perks up as the food is brought into the house. Sonrisa makes her way to the radio, turning it on, causing Sensato-Que Lo Que to fill the room, playing throughout the scene.

Montage footage of their small birthday party rolls.

Sonrisa goes to Miguel, takes his iPad and places it on the table, grabbing him by the arm-

Miguel:

(whining in protest) But, Mama, I was playing a game.

Sonrisa:

You can play that anytime. It's my birthday, and I want to dance with mis ninos. (She scoops up Marcos.) You want to dance with your mother, don't you, Marcos?

She tickles him. Steve holds his hand out toward Anita, who shyly smiles.

Steve:

Miss Colombiana, shall we?

She happily joins him on the kitchen floor, where all five people dance around. Show them all enjoying pizza slices and hot wings, as Sonrisa pours Steve a shot of tequila, and Marcos reaches for it, to the enjoyment of all as Steve covers the shot glass quickly, and looks at everybody bewildered, saying...

Steve:

(teasingly) Y'all think it's funny, but, he reached for that like he knows what he was about to get into. (He playfully pokes Marcos in the stomach, making him laugh.) Ain't that right?

Everybody smiles or laughs as Steve empties the shot glass.

Fade into them playing poker for candy, and Steve loses while holding Marcos.

Steve:

(feigning shocked realization) Aww, I see what's going on, here. It's a family hustle. Send Marcos to be all cute and soften me up. Then the mother deals the cards.

Sonrisa simulates hurt feelings by gasping and raising her hands to her chest.

Steve:

And the kids win, again. That's it!

He gets up and playfully puts Anita and Sonrisa in headlocks as Miguel jumps on his back. They all collapse into a pile on the floor, while Marcos eats candy from a mound on the table.

Steve:

Bunch of cheaters, I figured y'all out.

Sonrisa:

It's not our fault you can't play cards.

They all laugh as the scene fades into late night. All three children sleep on the couch as Sonrisa and Steve finish cleaning up, placing the last of the trash in a bag. Sonrisa drops a blanket on the kids. Steve wraps his arms around her waist from behind and kisses her cheek.

Steve:

They're beautiful, mi amor.

Sonrisa:

Thank you. And they took to you better than they've taken to anyone I've ever brought home. (Turning to face him, they kiss.) You know, I have one more present for you, papi.

Steve:

I was going to say the same thing to you.

She tries to lead him to the bedroom, but he leads her to the kitchen.

Sonrisa:

Let's go to the bed.

Steve:

Follow me.

Sonrisa:

I've been warned about following the Devil.

He lowers his gaze as she feigns reluctance by offering little resistance.

Steve:

Don't you trust me?

She only smiles as they enter the kitchen. Steve sits in a chair and pats the table in a gesture for Sonrisa to sit in front of him. Sonrisa looks toward the children with a look of apprehension on her face-

Sonrisa:

(wide-eyed) Mis ninos.

Steve:

(Pulling her close to him, he slides his right hand between her thighs, rubbing her already moist clitoris.) I won't make any noise if you don't. Besides, it feels like you're more than ready to me.

He sticks his tongue into her mouth before she can protest, while guiding her, picking her up slightly, sitting her on the table, raising her skirt to her hips, exposing her womanhood as she spreads her legs. Denual-A Solas plays as Steve begins to perform cunnilingus. Gasping and holding Steve's head in place, Sonrisa ignores her fallen shoulder straps as they slowly expose her breasts.

She grabs the edge of the table with both hands and scoots her hips closer to Steve's face, as an orgasm rocks her, she pulls a small chunk of wood from the table. Breathing heavily, she tells Steve…

Sonrisa:

Papi, give it to me, now, mi amor.

She leans and speedily undoes his belt and pants, grabbing him, and eases his erection into her. She braces, biting her bottom lip, raising her left leg on top of Steve's right shoulder as he pounds away, kissing him the entire time.

Steve:

You know why us Tauros belong together?

Sonrisa:

92

(through soft moans) Why's that, papi?

Steve:

'Cuz we fuck like the bulls we are.

They kiss.

Sonrisa:

Give me a nino, mi amor, give me your child.

Steve:

That's why we're doing this, ain't it?

He strokes a few more times and exhales heavily as he ejaculates into Sonrisa. She kisses him repeatedly.

Sonrisa:

I love feeling you splash into me.

Steve:

I love splashing into you, babygirl.

He pulls his pants up and sits back in the chair. Sonrisa looks into living room, seeing the children still asleep, and sits in his lap. They share a kiss.

Sonrisa:

Happy Birthday, papi.

Steve:

Happy Birthday, mami. (He reaches into his pocket, pulling out a ring box.) I have another.

Sonrisa gasps, placing her hands over her mouth.

Sonrisa:

Mi amor, it's too much.

Steve:

So, you don't want me to ask you to marry me?

Tears run down her cheeks like a waterfall as she leans it into his neck.

Steve:

(holding her face to look at him, teasing her) Do you know how many bottles I had to break before I found a piece that looked like a flawless diamond?

She slaps his arm and he dries the streaks from her face, only making room for fresh tears.

Sonrisa:

Mi marido (my husband), I had all but given up on ever getting married, I thought I was destined to raise mis ninos by myself, working in a sleazy bar until I got too old and my looks faded. Put it on me, mi amor.

She offers her left hand, and Steve graces her ring finger with the diamond.

Steve:

I've never really had standout birthdays, either. But, two of your most significant birthdays are complete horror stories. I know this won't totally erase the pain and memories, but, we can at least start making our own beautiful memories. On my birthday, I'm older, you see.

Sonrisa:

(smiling as she studies her ring) Mi Diablito, Mi Viejo (My Little Devil, My Old Man), I love you, so much, mi amor.

Steve:

I love you, too, baby.

They kiss and he pinches her butt. She squeals, jumping slightly.

Sonrisa:

(smiling) You pinched me!

Steve:

I was making sure I wasn't dreaming.

Sonrisa:

You're supposed to pinch you.

Steve:

That makes no sense, whatsoever. Why would I pinch me, when the most beautiful woman in the world is sitting right on my lap, with her tight little booty? (He gives it a squeeze, and she smiles and kisses him.)

Sonrisa:

My own little devil.

Steve:

Plus, I pinched you, to make sure that you're real.

She coos, snuggling into him, and they kiss.

Sonrisa:

Mi Diablito says and does all of the right things. This is by far, the best day of my life, mi amor.

Steve:

I'm glad I could be a part of it, and share it with you, because, this is the happiest day of my life as well. What would you like to do, now?

Sonrisa:

Let's go sleep on the couch with our ninos.

They go to the couch. Sonrisa lies behind Anita, who leans into her chest. Steve sits behind Miguel, but has to pick Marcos up to do so. Once he's seated, he sits Marcos in his lap. Miguel stretches his legs onto Anita's lap, leaning into Steve, while Marcos gets comfortable in his lap.

Sonrisa smiles at Steve as she watches this scene, a tear finding its way down her cheek. Once everyone is settled, Steve holds out his right hand toward her, she extends her left hand to his. They interlock fingers and say to one another…

Steve:

Happy Birthday, mi reina (my queen).

Sonrisa:

Happy Birthday, mi rey (my king).

Scene 12-Daddy Yankee-La Noche De Los 2 plays throughout this montage:

Show Sonrisa introducing Steve to her eight friends, swatting their hands away as they either rub, or attempt to rub his shoulders or chest. Sonrisa wraps her right arm around his left, and thrust her left hand at them, flaunting her engagement ring. They all look on with wide-eyed, slack-jawed envy, as they stare unbelievingly at the ring.

Anita runs in, flashing the diamond earrings at them.

Anita:

Look at what else he got her.

The ladies all gasp audibly, throwing their hands into the air, clearly incredulous at Sonrisa's fortune.

Bethany:

You can have more than one wife, papi.

Rosalita:

Or, you can just come over anytime you want to.

Sonrisa swats at them with a scowl on her face, causing them to laugh. She stares at them, never breaking eye contact as she pulls Steve to her, and hungrily sticks her tongue into his mouth, while placing his hands on her behind, turning the tables on her friends, as they now frown and playfully curse her.

Fade to Sonrisa's Bridal Shower/Bachelorette Party. Sonrisa dons her veil with Sara and Ilanny on either side of her. She suddenly bursts into tears and Ilanny and Sara rapidly wipe them away.

Sara:

Que pasa, chica?

Sonrisa:

I'm just so happy. I had all but given up on ever getting married.

Her friends and Anita all gather around her, comforting her, as Rosalita hands her a shot glass with something brown in it-

Rosalita:

No tears, chica, drink up, it's a celebration.

Sonrisa downs the liquid, grimaces as she swallows, and they all scream, throwing their hands up.

Meanwhile: At Steve's bachelor party, he, Freddie, Miguel, Marcos, and Freddie's four brothers, Raul, Costas, Franco, and Johnny, sit around a table, waiting on Miguel to down a shot of tequila.

Steve:

Come on, Miggy, it's now or never.

Costas:

Just swallow hard and don't think about it, Miggy.

Miguel slowly raises the glass to his lips as the men all inch toward him in anticipation. Miguel swiftly pours the alcohol into his mouth and swallows, squinting and taking huge breaths while holding his hand to his chest. The men all laugh as Miguel reaches for his Coca-Cola, greedily chasing the tequila. Marcos reaches for the tequila bottle, causing the men to burst into a fresh fit of laughter.

The knock on the door causes the men to all stare at it enthusiastically. The door swings open, revealing three male strippers, and the ladies all scream in delight as they enter and immediately do their jobs. Anita is pleasantly frozen as the ladies all enjoy her innocence.

Meanwhile: Two beautiful, big-breasted strippers dance for the gentlemen. Franco looks at one of them and nods her toward Miguel. She dances her way to him. His eyes widen as she leans toward him, breasts swinging inches from his face. She uses her index finger to lift his face to look at her. She pecks his lips and he exhales heavily, causing the men to laugh. She wiggles her breasts in his face, and takes his hands, placing both of them on her nipples, squeezing them simultaneously. Miguel's mouth opens slowly as the men all laugh. Both ladies grab Steve by his arms and lead him to a chair. Marcos reaches for one of the ladies with both hands, squeezing his fingers.

Meanwhile: Sonrisa sits in a chair while three male strippers dance around her, making her blush. One stripper bends slightly in her face, saying…

Stripper:

You have to slap it if you want it to move.

Sonrisa slaps it lightly.

Stripper:

That isn't going to do it.

Sonrisa reaches for a shot glass, downs the tequila, and slaps the stripper's behind roughly as she gets up and starts dancing with the stripper, and all of the ladies follow suit, making it a true party.

Meanwhile: Steve sits in a chair with one stripper's bare ass and vagina in his face, buttocks clapping while her hips move left to right, while the other stripper lays her breasts on top of his bald head, smooshing them together.

The stripper in front of him raises up, asking him…

Stripper:

Want to go into the bedroom, with us?

Steve:

As much as I would like to, scratch that, love to, I have to respectfully decline. But the fellas…

They waste no time as Freddie and his brothers all walk the ladies into the bedroom, leaving Steve and the boys to entertain themselves.

Montage footage ends.

Act 5-Scene 13: July 27. 8:03 A.M.

Elvis Crespo-La Novia Bella plays throughout the montage:

Anita wakes up first and shakes Sonrisa awake.

Anita:

Mama, aren't you excited?!

Sonrisa:

You know that I am, hija. Happy Birthday, princess.

Anita:

You're getting married on my birthday.

They both squeal, causing the other eight ladies to stir themselves awake.

Talia:

Mis amigas, one of us is finally getting married!!!

They all explode into a celebratory fit of laughter and wails. Meanwhile: 9:30 A.M. In the hotel room, the men all eat pizza slices from the night before as Steve says…

Steve:

Y'all don't think she's going to leave me at the altar, do you?

Freddie:

Listen to me. Before you came into her life, she was working in my club, single, raising three ninos. (He rubs the tops of Miguel's and Marcos' heads). Only way she leaves you standing at the altar, is if Donald Trump kidnaps her and they fly off in a helicopter.

The adults laugh.

Raul:

It's just nerves, amigo. You've been trapped.

Johnny:

If anything, she's probably worrying about you ditching her.

Meanwhile: 10:27 A.M.: The ladies all run around, getting dressed, scurrying around, doing each other's hair and makeup, trying to calm a nervous Sonrisa.

Sonrisa:

( almost crying, in a panic) What if he panics and leaves me at the altar?

Penelope:

You have to calm down, chica. He loves you.

Carmen:

The way you two look at each other, I'm so jealous.

Anita:

They're right, mamita. What you said you two felt when you first met…

Helena:

…Like something out of a fairytale.

Bethany:

And, let's not forget, the most important thing…

All eight ladies sound off in unison…

All eight ladies:

THE ORGASMS!!!

They all laugh as Sonrisa smiles at the shocked reaction on Anita's face.

Meanwhile: 11:01 A.M.: The men are all dressed in all-white tuxedoes, with white hats and white shoes. Steve stands Marcos up after putting on his shoes and looks at his groomsmen.

Raul:

Amigo, I just met you, and, I feel honored that you chose us to stand by you today.

Steve:

I'm glad you feel that way. Being new to Colombia, once you all didn't rob me, I knew you were some good guys.

The men laugh.

Freddie:

Mi hermano, you're taking one of my best employees. The good news is, you're taking Sonrisa, and rescuing her. If anyone deserves anything better, it's her.

Franco:

It's Judgement Day, mis amigos, let's get this man to the executioner.

The men laugh. Steve looks at Miguel.

Steve:

You ready to walk your mother down the aisle?

Miguel:

Si.

Steve grabs the back of his head and places their foreheads together.

Steve:

We're family, now, hijo. Blood. I'm here to stay.

Miguel:

I know, papito.

Steve kisses his forehead, and pulls Marcos into him, kissing his forehead.

Steve:

Let's do this, fellas.

Meanwhile: 11:23 A.M. The ladies all gawk at Sonrisa in her wedding dress.

Helena:

Let me take your place, Sonrisa?

Sara:

You look so precious, amiga.

Ilanny and Bethany look out of a window and see the men exiting cars-

Bethany:

Here they come. They look so sexy in their tuxedoes.

All of the ladies rush the window to share the sight of the groom and his groomsmen.

Sonrisa:

Look at mi marido and mis.ninos, they look so handsome.

A tear wells up in her eyes and her maid of honor, Anita, tells her…

Anita:

Mama, don't cry.

Sonrisa stiffens and beams.

Sonrisa:

You're right. Mi marido is here. I'm about to become his wife. Let's do this.

They all huddle up and squeal in delight.

Scene 14- Steve stands at the altar, groomsmen lined up behind him, smallest to the tallest. Every bridesmaid, with the exception of his stepdaughter Anita, eyes him. Steve pulls Freddie to him.

Steve:

Who are all of these people?

Freddie:

They're all of our families.

Steve:

Awww, okay. Just like in the States, you Latinos never miss an opportunity to party.

Freddie:

And, a wedding and a Quinceañera! Good luck keeping us away. There's going to be people at the reception that we don't know.

Steve:

The more, the merrier.

Freddie slaps Steve's back a few times and returns to his spot.

The audience rises when the priest pushes a button on an MP3 player, and Karen Martello-Besame Asi blares from the speakers, as Miguel and Sonrisa stand at the entrance, arm in arm, and, to the amusement of everyone, dance down the aisle to the song.

Steve can only smile as he watches his bride-to-be dance down the aisle, with a vibrant Miguel, whose gyrations garner laughter from the audience. Steve and Sonrisa lock eyes momentarily, smile, and mouth the words 'I love you' to one another. He looks toward Anita, who notices, smiles, and mouths 'Happy Birthday' to her. She flashes all thirty-two teeth at him, prompting the same reaction from him.

The priest stops the music as Sonrisa and Miguel approach the podium. Sonrisa kisses Miguel on the cheek. Miguel goes and takes his place behind Marcos. Steve reaches toward Sonrisa with his left hand, Sonrisa takes it with her right, and Special Effects shows sparks between them, once they touch, the sparks shoot to their hearts, making them beat faster. They both smile brightly, knowing that they both felt the sensation. They stare into each other's eyes.

Steve:

You look so beautiful, baby, I love you.

Sonrisa:

You look very handsome, yourself. I love you, too.

Priest:

Now, that's how you start a wedding.

Everyone laughs.

Priest:

I understand that the bride and groom would like to recite their own vows?

Sonrisa:

Yes, we would, Father, and, I would like to go first.

She and Steve face one another and hold hands.

Sonrisa:

Mi amor, I love you. I love you, so much, and more than you'll ever know. I know I've thoroughly explained the horrors of my past, but, you'll never fully understand just how much light you've brought into my life, in so little time, after all of these years. (She cries. Steve attempts to dry her eyes, but Sonrisa hold his hands in place.) Let me cry, mi amor. I have to get this out. Despite the feelings we felt physically when we first met, and you doing what you did the first night we met, your heart is the reason that I love you, and your actions are the reason that I know you love me. I know that you weren't just an average American, coming to Colombia, looking for any Latina, because you met me, I'm thirty with three kids, and, you could've had any other, younger childless woman.

Her bridesmaids collectively utter their affirmations, to the playful annoyance of the bride, and the amusement of every witness. Sonrisa turns to them and berates them quickly.

Sonrisa:

Callate, malditas, Callate!

They wave and wink, blowing kisses at Steve, who only grins and nods his head.

Sonrisa:

(looking angrily at her bridesmaids) But you chose me! (She looks at Steve, smiling.) Every day you show me just why I held on and never took my own life. I told you about my past, you stayed. I told you I had kids, and, not only did you stay, you proposed, immediately started taking care of us, and are marrying me, in three months. If you're not the man I've been praying for since I was fifteen, there is no man. I've never felt this way in my life. Thirty years old and I'm just now experiencing what I used to read about in books. I feel like I'm going to explode from happiness. You're my first love, my only love, and last love. Deep down, I know that no one else will ever compare to you. I love you, Mi Diablito. I love you.

The camera pans through the audience, showing a stunned crowd, some in tears. Anita cries as the rest of the bridesmaids look on, smiling slightly.

Priest:

( looking at Steve) I'd hate to have to follow that act.

Steve:

Padre, I got this. (He clears his throat, playfully long, to the amusement of everyone but his bride, who swats his arm.) Aw, I'm sorry, baby. Okay, look good, and you can cook good. You may kiss the groom.

Steve puckers his lips out far, closes his eye and leans toward Sonrisa, who scowls playfully and taps his cheek with her fingers, bringing him to reality, as everyone laughs uproariously.

Sonrisa:

(chiding him smiling) Diablo!

They smile at one another.

Steve:

Seriously, mi amor, I love you. I've never felt what you've been bringing out of me ever since I first laid eyes on you, ever before in my life. That's how I know that it's real. I can't say that you put something in my drink, or took my blood and did voodoo on me, but, I can say, without a doubt in my mind, that you did cast a spell on me, because you did it with your eyes the first time we looked at one another.

Sonrisa's eyes overflow with tears.

Steve:

Like I told you that night on the beach, I don't know how life could treat something as beautiful and precious as you, so horrible for twenty-nine to thirty years, only to have you emerge from those depths, more beautiful than ever. The only reason I know it can be done, is because I'm looking at a real life example. You always tell me how lucky you are to have waited for, and finding me. That I'm your first love, and the first person to bring you happiness. That would put pressure on any other man, yet, it just gives me bravado, making me feel confident that I can be such a source of everything good, to someone as beautiful as you. And, I can't wait to spend the rest of my life, bringing you that happiness, and proving to you exactly why we were made for one another.

Sonrisa's crying gets slightly audible as the camera pans the audience, showing many men and women in tears.

Sonrisa:

Keep going, mi amor.

Steve:

I plan to. I find it coincidental that, you were orphaned, I was orphaned, I made my share of orphans, I find you, fall in love, and now we both are going to raise two orphans ourselves. I only hope that, they use our example and end up a thousand times better for it.

Show Anita and Miguel in a split-screen, both crying and being comforted by the person closest to them. Steve continues.

110

Steve:

And, I need you to know this, I never believed in marriage, because, I used to look at other couples, and see that they didn't take those vows serious at all. Through sickness and health, I'm bound to you. If you end up with cancer, brain damage, or paralyzed; I'm taking care of you. Good times and bad. No matter what happens, you're stuck with me, now, so, good luck to you.

Everyone laughs.

Steve:

And, finally, for richer or poorer. I just told you that you're stuck with me. Am I stuck with you, no matter what?

Sonrisa nods in the affirmative.

Steve:

If I go broke, can I still get you out of your clothes?

The crowd laughs as Sonrisa smiles and swats his chest.

Sonrisa:

Diablo!

Steve:

I didn't hear a no, so, let's do this.

Steve reaches under her veil, drying her tears away as she smiles at him.

Priest:

And, let me just say that, of all the weddings I've performed, those were the best, most entertaining vows that I've ever heard. I couldn't've done it better if I tried. (He turns his attention to the groomsmen.) Rings, gentlemen?

All of them pat their pockets and blazers as if they've forgotten the rings. Sonrisa's eyes bulge in irritation as Steve reaches into his coat pocket, saying to the priest and Sonrisa…

Steve:

Look at that bunch of bandits, you think I'd let them hold these?

Everyone laughs as he pulls the box containing the rings from his pocket.

Priest:

(to Sonrisa) Looks as if you've found yourself a jokester?

Sonrisa:

(smiling, touching Steve's face) He's Mi Diablito, Padre. I love him.

Steve:

( returning her smile) I love you, too, mi angelita.

Priest:

On that note, do you, Sonrisa Ciela Jerez, take this man to be your lawfully wedded husband?

Sonrisa:

I do. (She slides the ring onto Steve's finger.)

Priest:

And do you, Steven Marcus Davis, take this woman to be your lawfully wedded wife?

Steve:

I do. (He places the ring onto Sonrisa's finger.)

Priest:

You may kiss the bride.

They obey as Steve raises her veil, leans in, and they share their first kiss as man and wife. Special effects show their hearts beating in unison, picking up speed, and getting louder. They end their kiss with a few pecks, smiling at each other, saying-

Everyone rises, applauding momentarily, admiring the newlyweds. Steve raises his hands, requesting silence.

Steve:

I love you, mi Angelita.

Sonrisa:

I love you too, Mi Diablito.

Everyone rises, applauding momentarily, admiring the newlyweds. Steve raises his hands, requesting silence.

Steve:

This wedding has officially become a Quinceañera!!! (He looks at Anita.) Happy Birthday, mi amor.

Anita:

(beaming) Thank you, Steve.

Steve:

Now, can we party, or what?!!!

Scene 15-2:14 P.M.: Costas' voice booms from speakers as he DJs the Reception/Quinceañera.

Costas:

Ladies and Gentlemen, in order to start this party off right, dancing together for the first time as husband and wife, please welcome to the dance floor, Mr. and Mrs. Steven Marcus Davis!!!

The entire crowd rises and applauds the couple as they take to the center of the dance floor. Steve and Sonrisa now wear tennis shoes.

Costas:

Before we start, allow me to say congratulations to the newlyweds, who, I've noticed, must intend to dance all night, having changed shoes…

Everybody laughs.

Costas:

…and, Happy Birthday to their fifteen-year-old daughter, Anita, looking beautiful in her powder blue dress, tiara, and Miss Colombiana sash.

Anita stands shyly, smile wide, and waves to the crowd as they applaud her. She looks at Steve and Sonrisa, who look back at each other, and waves at them as they return the gesture.

Costas:

Now, the groom should never forget his daughter's birthday, and most definitely not his anniversary.

Everyone laughs.

Costas:

Once the first song ends, we're in birthday party mode. So, without further ado…

Eli-Every time We Touch booms from the speakers as Steve and Sonrisa embrace, smile at one another after listening to the words, and share a kiss, then immediately start swaying to the song.

Sonrisa:

The girl knows what she's talking about.

Steve:

I figured you'd like this song.

As the song goes on, they get more and more into their dance, to the enjoyment of their guests. They briefly separate, and Sonrisa lowers her gaze seductively at her husband, saunters backwards while swinging her hips side to side beckoning him to follow her with her finger, he obeys. She stops, turns her back to him, looks back at him, grinning, and sticks her behind out at him. He acts as if he'll squeeze it with both hands, and she turns to face him, wagging her finger in the negative, and playfully touches his cheek with her fingertips in a mock slap. Steve feigns being in pain as the crowd claps and laughs. Sonrisa puts her arms around his neck, and this time, he squeezes her behind, and they kiss passionately to the cheers of their guests. They put their forehead together and share a smile, dancing out the song.

The song goes off, and the couple wave to an applauding crowd. Sonrisa and Steve beckon their daughter to the dance floor. Anita runs to them, smile shining brightly, giggling as she makes her way to her parents.

Anita:

Mama, Steve, congratulations. You two look so sweet together.

Sonrisa:

Thank you, hija.

Steve:

Happy Birthday, Miss Colombiana.

Anita smiles at him. Costas' voice erupts from the speakers.

Costas:

LET'S GET PHYSICAL!!!

Olga Tanon-Todo Lo Que Sube, Baja, plays throughout the first half of the montage, as the dance floor is instant packed.

116

Overhead shots show the party from every angle.

On the dance floor, show Miguel and Marcos dancing with the bridesmaids.

Show the bridesmaids surrounding Steve, dancing up on him, and Bethany and Talia trapping him, with Bethany backing her behind onto his midsection. Sonrisa comes out of nowhere, waving her finger in Bethany's face, and uses her hands to fan away her bridesmaids. She turns to Steve, saying…

Sonrisa:

Querido, don't let them do that.

Steve:

I'm sorry, baby.

Sonrisa:

It's not you I'm worried about.

Steve:

Okay, mi amor. Let's have fun.

Sonrisa turns, facing her bridesmaids, and places her backside onto Steve's midsection, grinning devilishly at them, as they scowl at her.

A split-screen shows Sonrisa and her bridesmaids, Steve and his groomsmen, all lined up at the bar, simultaneously taking back shots.

Show Anita dancing with her brothers.

Show the groomsmen all tossing Steve into the air, catching him, and repeating.

Show Sonrisa holding and swaying a sleeping Marcos, while she dances with Miguel.

It's now dark outside at 8:38 P.M., when the song fades into Pitbull-Give Me Everything (Tonight).

Show Steve and Sonrisa cutting into their wedding cake at the same time Anita blows out the candles on her birthday cake, when Miguel sticks both of his fingers into the icing on each cake, eating the icing from the tips.

Show a few people approaching the bride, groom, and Anita, handing them envelopes, and they put them into a bag that a groomsmen and a bridesmaid hold.

Show Sonrisa holding her hands over Anita's eyes, as Raul and Franco carry a box that's about six feet in height, and three feet on all four sides, wrapped with a giant bow on top of it. Sonrisa removes her hands and Anita gasps with excitement.

Steve:

Happy Birthday, sweetheart.

Sonrisa:

Happy Birthday, nina.

Anita wraps either arm around both of their waists.

Anita:

Thank you, so much, what is it?!

Steve:

Clothes, makeup, shoes, a phone, some other trinkets.

Costas' voice booms from the speakers.

Costas:

Attention, attention. Would the birthday girl and her father please report to the center of the dance floor?

Sonrisa:

(feigning jealousy, playfully holding Steve back when Anita grabs his other arm) You can't dance with Mi marido.

They all smile as Sonrisa kisses both of their cheeks, and they make their way to the center of the dance floor. When they get there, Steve signals to Anita with both arms, and the crowd claps as Anita spins one time, smiling from ear to ear.

Costas:

This song was chosen by Steve personally, dedicated to his new daughter, on her birthday.

The bridesmaids all surround Sonrisa as her eyes begin to tear up.

K-Rose-Just the Way You Are plays, as Steve and Anita assumes the dancing position.

Anita:

Congratulations, once again, Steve.

Steve:

Thank you. And, Happy Birthday, once again, Miss Colombiana.

She smiles and blushes as they start their dance. After the song plays a verse and the chorus, Show Sonrisa crying, being comforted by her bridesmaids.

Sara:

What's wrong, chica, you're supposed to be happy?!

Sonrisa:

I am. I just can't believe that, I'm married, and Anita is having a Quinceañera as big and beautiful as this.

Anita dries tears from her eyes as she smiles. Steve helps her clear tears away and pulls her head to his chest.

Steve:

I take it those are happy tears?

Anita:

Si.

Miguel looks at his crying mother and sister, saying loud enough for his mother and her bridesmaids to hear...

Miguel:

Women, always crying. (He looks at the ladies and puts his fists to his eyes, mimicking crying.)

They all playfully berate him, Sonrisa pushes his head, and he laughs, running away.

Meanwhile: Outside: Vibora and his men stand at the entrance to the banquet hall, looking in on Steve and Anita as they dance.

Vibora:

The disrespect is astounding.

He turns his head slightly, staring at Sonrisa.

Vibora:

(with a hint of malice in his voice) The bride looks more beautiful than ever, though.

A chorus of agreement from his men.

Oblivious to the presence of Vibora and his men, Sonrisa stares at her new husband lovingly as he dances with a little girl that she found abandoned on the street, eating out of the trash, and she can't help but cry.

An overhead shot of Steve and Anita dancing ends the scene as it fades to black.

PART 1 ENDS

# Part 2:
# The Bad

ACT 5: SCENE 16 - 1 MONTH LATER-9:13 A.M.

Tito El Bambino-Tu Olor plays as the camera briefly shows the five main rooms of the house, starting with the kitchen, living room, the boys bedroom, and Anita's room, all decked out with up-to-date flat-screen televisions, computers, video games, refrigerator, stove, and washer/ dryer. A totally different home from the subpar equipped house of a few months ago.

The kids are lined up by height, right ears to their parents' door, softly giggling as they listen to the sounds of lovemaking.

On the other side of the door, Sonrisa has both legs on Steve's shoulders, her hands gripping the headboard, as Steve pounds away. They exchange a heated kiss as Steve releases his load. Sonrisa smiles and rubs his face.

Sonrisa:

Mi amor, Mi Diablito, mi toro, mi marido, I love you.

Steve:

I love you, too, mi angelita.

Steve lies on his side and Sonrisa turns to face him. They embrace each other.

Steve:

You know your ninos are right outside, listening, don't you?

Sonrisa:

(laughing shyly) No! Our ninos.

Steve:

I heard them giggling one day. Then, I turned around and could see the shadows from their feet.

They both laugh and share a kiss.

Sonrisa;

All ninos do that.

Steve:

I know. I'm just letting you know so that we can get a little louder.

Sonrisa:

(slapping his shoulder) Diablo!

They laugh and kiss.

Sonrisa:

I want to go shopping with Anita today.

Steve:

Okay. Take them all, please?

Sonrisa:

Girls only.

Outside the door, the kids march to the kitchen.

Miguel:

They're through. I'm hungry.

Anita:

(picking up Marcos) Me and Mama are going to have a girls' day.

In the bedroom…

Steve:

What do you girls talk about, all day, every day?

Sonrisa:

Boys and tampons…

Steve:

(covering his ears) LALALALALALALA!!! I'm sorry I asked.

Sonrisa laughs and tickles him, making him drop his arms.

Sonrisa:

Are you going to give us some money?

Steve:

Y'all got money.

Sonrisa:

But we need more.

Steve:

Since when did wives start spending all of their husbands' money?

Sonrisa:

Since forever, papi.

Steve:

I never heard that. I'm going to have to check into that.

Sonrisa reaches between his legs, slowly stroking his penis and slides her tongue into his mouth.

Sonrisa:

Please, Mi Diablito? We girls just want to have fun.

Steve:

I'll think about it.

Sonrisa goes down and noisily places him into her mouth, which brings him to full tilt.

Steve:

Okay, I could probably give you about two or three more dollars.

Scene 17-1:31 P.M.: Wisin Y Yandel-No Dejemos Que Se Apague plays throughout the scene.

Sonrisa and Anita exit a beauty salon, sporting new hairdos, lightly made up, holding multiple shopping bags, laughing and talking.

Sonrisa:

And, tomorrow, I have a photographer coming to the house to take a family photo, then I'm going to have a painter paint a giant picture of us.

Anita:

Mamita, take a breath, you're going a mile a minute.

Sonrisa:

I'm just so happy, princesa, so happy.

An all-white stretch Bentley limousine, with all tinted windows, pulls up alongside of them. The window rolls down, revealing Vibora's sinister grin.

Sonrisa:

I spoke too soon.

Vibora:

Pretty ones, you both look gorgeous. (to Sonrisa) This must be your hija, the one whose Quinceañera I wasn't invited to. Please, allow me to give you two a ride home.

Sonrisa:

No, thank you.

Chico and Carlos both exit the limo from the  other side, approach the ladies, the trunk opens-

Vibora:

It wasn't a question, Pretty One.

Anita is clearly apprehensive, not knowing who any of these men are.

Anita:

(to Sonrisa) Mama, who is he, and what's going on?!

Sonrisa:

It's okay, mi amor.

Chico and Carlos reach and take the bags from the ladles, when Vibora steps out, wearing black wingtips, white slacks, and a black button-up shirt, with the two top buttons undone, and signals with his left hand for the ladies to enter.

Vibora:

Ladies, your chariot.

Sonrisa, poorly masking her anger, and Anita, not at all masking her trepidation, reluctantly enter the automobile. Once everyone is inside the vehicle, it moves. Once in motion, Anita holds Sonrisa's hand and stares at Vibora, who notices, but remains gracious. Sonrisa speaks English, Vibora Espanol.

Vibora:

Little Pretty One, you don't have to be nervous.

Sonrisa:

One should always remain cautious when confronted by a Vibora.

Vibora smiles away her attitude.

Vibora:

Ah, Pretty One, always feisty.

Sonrisa:

What do you want, Don Jefe?

Vibora:

I only wish to tell you congratulations on your blessed wedding, and to wish your daughter a happy birthday. (He smiles at Sonrisa menacingly.) A girl's fifteenth birthday is a very special time in her life. Do you remember your fifteenth birthday, Pretty One?

Visualize- The images of Sonrisa's mother, Sylvia, with her brains blown out on her bed, and the four men having their way with her, smack her vividly, bringing tears to her eyes, which Sonrisa channels into rage, but keeps her tone as calm as possible. Anita notices this and her eyes well up as she grips her mother's hand.

Sonrisa:

Si, I do remember my fifteenth birthday.

Vibora:

So do I, Pretty One, so do I. Please stop speaking to me in English. You know my English isn't very good, and, I find it somewhat disrespectful.

Sonrisa:

(continuing in English) I apologize, if you find my speaking English disrespectful, but, I find your presence sickening.

Vibora:

Always the fighter, just like your sign, the bull.

Vibora is in Sonrisa's face in a flash, with his left hand around her throat, taking after his moniker.

Vibora:

You listen to me, bitch!

Anita reaches out and grabs his arm.

Anita:

Let go of my mother, imbecile!

Vibora:

(to Chico) Please, gently subdue Anita. (to Sonrisa) Pretty One, I asked you nicely to respect me, in my car, when I'm only trying to be nice and take you ladies home. Now, I've noticed a sense of superiority ever since your American nigger came and rescued you and your stray children. But, don't ever forget, you may be his wife, but you'll always be my bitch, Pretty One. Always!

He releases her and takes his original seat. Anita and Sonrisa console each other. Vibora goes back to gentleman mode.

Vibora:

Now, ladies, if we can continue our conversation, without all of this malice, and, in Espanol, please?

Sonrisa:

(en Espanol) It's funny how, before I met Steve, when I was poor, working in a nightclub, and raising three kids by myself, for almost nine years, you didn't check on me once. Not once! But, now, that I have a husband, a good husband, now you slither your way back into my life. It's almost as if, the biggest drug lord in all of Colombia, has nothing better to do, with all that your money affords you, than to make an innocent girl, whom you forced into prostitution, and held captive most of her life, miserable. What does that say about you?

Vibora simply stares out of his window.

Sonrisa:

How long do I have to be cursed with your presence, for something I never did to you, and suffer for a father that I've never known? My father and uncles couldn't've possibly stolen that much from you. Look at you now. Not unless, after all of this money you've made from all of the misery you and your precious cocaine have spread, you can't be happy? And, if that's the case, why are you doing all of this?

Sonrisa chuckles to herself.

Sonrisa:

Why don't you do like all of the other kingpins, and go to jail or get massacred? Miserable son-of-a-bitch!

The car stops.

Vibora:

Pretty ones, your stop.

Chico and Carlos exit with the ladies closely in their wake, both of them not being able to contain their anxiousness in being able to exit the vehicle. Sonrisa stops short, motioning for Anita to go ahead of her.

Sonrisa:

Thanks for the ride that we didn't ask for.

She briskly exits, standing to a waiting Carlos, who is handing her, her bags. She thanks him as she takes them from him, he nods and enters the automobile after Chico. Once the door closes, it pulls away.

Anita:

Mama, who was he to you?

Sonrisa:

Someone I was hoping you'd never have to know, and someone I never wanted to have to tell you about. And, speaking of not telling people things…

Anita:

I won't tell Steve, Mama.

Sonrisa:

Promise me.

Anita:

I promise, mamita.

Sonrisa turns away from Anita, drops her bags, and vomits. Anita releases her bags and comes to her mother's aid.

Anita:

What's wrong, are you okay/?!

Sonrisa:

I'm pregnant. Don't tell your father that, either. Promise.

They both smile awkwardly.

Anita:

I promise.

Meanwhile: 3:30 P.M.: Plan B-Si No Le Contesto plays in Freddie's club, which is virtually empty, when Vibora, Chico, and Carlos waltz in.

Freddie straightens and puts on a bartender's grin-

Freddie:

Vibora, finally come out of your castle, heh, mingle with the poor folks?

Vibora:

Not at all, Freddie. Not at all. Just came to let you know that, I'm going to be commandeering your establishment from here on out, I need some place for a new shipment of girls that I have coming in to work. And, why build a new building, when one already stands?

Freddie eyes him with a slight recalcitrance.

Vibora:

That's the second time today that I've gotten that look from someone.

Freddie:

If you had a dollar, huh?

It's Vibora's turn to wear a contemptuous look.

Vibora:

I do, Freddie, I do. I've always liked you, Freddie, You and your brothers. Little do-gooders. I see you all have gotten really friendly with Sonrisa's new husband since he's been here.

Freddie:

He's a very good guy.

Vibora:

Any man that willingly marries a former whore with 3 bastards has to have some good in him.

Freddie:

If my memory serves me correctly, Sonrisa was forced into sexual slavery, no? To pay for a debt that wasn't hers? Only a true scumbag would do such a thing to an innocent girl.

Vibora:

Let the groom know that I'd like to have a word with him, if it's not too much to ask?

Freddie:

Will do, snake. I mean, Vibora.

Vibora and his men head for the door.

Vibora:

(turning to Freddie) I hope you're ready to make a lot of money.

Freddie:

Maybe not the way that I imagined, but, money is money.

Vibora:

That it is, Freddie. That it is.

The door swings shut, leaving Freddie to stare while he stews in his own anger.

Outside, Vibora brightens when he spots Steve approaching the establishment he just left, with Miguel and Marcos in tow.

Vibora:

(raising his hands) Steve, just the man I was looking for.

Steve:

(heavily sarcastically) Lucky me.

Vibora extends his right hand to Miguel, who shrinks back as Steve pulls him closer.

Steve:

Let's leave the kids out of this, shall we?

Vibora:

( looking slightly disrespected) As you wish.

Steve:

Miggy, take your brother home.

Miguel:

But, you said…

Steve:

It wasn't a request, Miggy. ( kneeling down to face him) This is serious, okay?

Miguel:

( returning his gaze) Okay.

Miguel takes Marcos' hand and heads home.

Steve stands, faces Vibora, Carlos, and Chico, as Chico opens the door to the vehicle, and Steve enters first, followed by the nefarious trio.

Alexis Y Fido-Rescate plays throughout the Scene.

Vibora sits directly across from Steve, with Chico to his left, while Carlos sits on Steve's right.

Vibora:

Let's cut to the chase, Steve. I didn't appreciate being disrespected by you and your new wife. Congratulations, by the way.

Steve:

I wasn't aware that my wife and I showed you any disrespect.

Vibora:

You all didn't invite me to the wedding, or the Quinceañera. Disrespected twice in one day.

Steve:

It was a very valid reason why you weren't invited.

Vibora:

Why's that?

Steve:

Because we didn't want you there.

 The men exchange measured glances. Vibora, never having anyone, let alone a black American stranger, address him thus, and Steve, having never held his tongue for anyone, are both stubbornly on guard,

Meanwhile: Miguel enters his home, holding Marcos by the hand. They both have some form of candy, which Sonrisa takes from them.

Sonrisa:

( kissing both of their cheeks) No, my children, you'll ruin your dinner Nita and I are cooking.

Miguel:

If Anita's cooking, can I just have my candy back?

Anita yells at him from the kitchen.

Anita:

Callate, Miggy!

Sonrisa:

( talking to Miguel while lifting Marcos) Where's your father?

Miguel:

Some man in a white limousine asked him to talk. He told me to bring Marcos home, and they drove off.

She and Anita both stare at each other with worry in their eyes. Miguel notices this immediately and asks…

Miguel:

( excited) What's wrong, and who was that rich man?!

Sonrisa:

Nobody, sweetheart. Go wash your hands and help me and your sister with dinner.

Miguel:

( pouting while he stomps softly into the kitchen) You never tell me anything.

Sonrisa:

( looking out of the living room window) I know, papi. I know.

Meanwhile: In the limo:

Vibora:

Why didn't you want me there, if I may ask?

Steve:

You already know exactly why that is. But, since you insist on playing this game, and dragging out this conversation, I'll tell you. First of all, you know that your very presence makes my wife want to vomit. I love her, so not only is it my job to do any and everything to prevent her from being unhappy, by extension, knowing what you did to her, makes me want to vomit. She hates your fucking guts. I don't know you to hate you, but, from what I've heard, I don't like you at all. From what she tells me, she hasn't physically laid eyes on you since you released her from that prison of a house of yours, that is, until the day she met me, which was nine years after her release date. Why do you think that is?

Steve pauses to let Vibora give an answer. Vibora just stares at Steve.

Steve:

I'll tell you why. Deep down, you're a sad, miserable man. Your father left you a legacy of cocaine, and a fortune acquired not only from that, but sex trafficking, murder, and untold misery. And, you're still not happy. Now, don't think that I'm knocking your hustle, by no means. I made my money without dealing in women. They liken robbers to vultures, which, I'll accept. Vultures eat dead bodies, I left dead bodies. Vultures eat what others won't, I do what others won't. But, two things for certain, I'll survive by any means available to me. And, if someone wronged me, I never took it out on their family and children, I dealt with that individual directly, not their kids. There is nothing macho about forcing babies into prostitution. I know guys where I'm from who'll turn you into a girl for doing that shit.

Vibora:

I have to stop this, now. I no longer have to extend our Colombian courtesy to you now, because you are no longer a tourist, but a Colombian, having married into this country, now, I'm going to treat you like I treat all of the other Colombians.

Steve:

You're the man. I get that, but, you have one problem.

Vibora:

What's that?

Steve:

I come from a place, where, everybody wanted to be the man, so we were all killing each other daily, trying to be the man.

Vibora:

You forget one thing.

Steve:

What's that?

This isn't Chicago.

Steve:

All the more reason for me to play that much harder, so I can shit on you on your home court. And, I may not be in Chicago, but, Chicago is still in me, and I'm still the man. And, last but not least, every day of my life, I've went to war with, and against, Latinos. You all may be better organized and equipped, but, a war is a war. Case in point...

Steve moves with celerity as he leans forward, pulling his gun from his spine, and shoots both Carlos and Chico two times in their foreheads, causing a chunk of brain matter to exit the backs of their heads, as blood paints the interior, Steve looks at Vibora, aiming at his head.

Steve:

You should invest into quicker, more alert men.

The car stops.

Vibora:

Your destination. Before you leave, you should kill me.

Steve:

I could tell you the same thing. But, we both know that your other goons know where you are, your driver has seen me, so, it wouldn't make much of a difference. Not to mention, I want to draw this out, see how this movie ends. What's war without an adversary?

Steve puts his gun away.

Steve:

You have a nice day.

Vibora:

You as well.

Steve exits the vehicle, but, not before hearing urine from Vibora's leg splash lightly onto the carpeted floor. Steve smiles at him, then closes the door behind him. Vibora curses himself as he rubs his urine-stained trousers, in a vain attempt to remove the stain, as well as his shame.

Scene 18: Steve enters the house to Marcos and Sonrisa greeting him. Marcos holds his hands up for Steve to pick him up. Steve obliges him as Sonrisa kisses his lips. She notices a red drop on his hand as he holds Marcos.

Sonrisa:

What's this?

Upon wiping, her eyes widen with recognition.

Sonrisa:

What happened, mi amor, are you okay?!

Steve:

Yes, chiquita, I'm cool. Not now, I don't want to scare the kids.

Sonrisa:

Go wash up and come eat. Anita and I cooked.

Steve:

( talking so Anita can hear him) Oh, you and Nita cooked, I knew I smelled something good!

Miguel never looks up from his iPad.

Miguel:

Well, it couldn't be Nita's cooking.

Sonrisa:

Be nice, Miggy.

Anita:

( talking so Miguel can hear her) I made sure I took extra special care of yours, hermanito (little brother).

Sonrisa stops the retort, admonishing them both.

Sonrisa:

Would you two please be nice, before we all sit down and eat?! Miggy, give me the iPad and go with your father and brother and wash your hands and face.

Miguel:

(protesting weakly) But, Mama, I—

Sonrisa:

( taking the iPad) But, nothing, bandito, go wash up. (She swats his behind with the iPad and tosses it on the couch.)

In the bathroom, Steve holds Marcos so that he can hold his hands under the faucet as Miguel soaps his hands.

Miguel:

Papa, who was that rich man? Mama won't tell me anything.

Steve:

Don't let the money fool you, nino. He's rich, but, he's not a good man. He's not a good man at all. Just because a person has money, doesn't mean that they're good.

Miguel:

So, he's a drug lord?

Steve:

Yes, Miggy, he's a drug lord. Don't tell your mother I told you that.

Steve winks at Miguel, and they smile.

At their dinner table, Marion-Sans Toi plays throughout the scene as a medley of their conversation is heard, slightly louder than the song.

Show Anita and Miguel acting as if they'll throw food at each other.

Steve:

Somebody could be eating that food you two are playing with. You both know that from personal experience.

They put the food back on the plates.

Steve:

Besides, that's what Marcos is for.

A small gob of rice hits Steve in his right eye, causing all to laugh, with the exception of Steve, who cleans his face.

Steve:

See what I mean.

He smiles, and the laughter resumes.

Show them listening to Anita.

Anita:

...and I want him to be mi novio.

Steve:

(winking at Miguel, who laughs) Good luck with having a boyfriend with me around.

Both ladies look at Steve, slightly shocked.

Sonrisa:

Why can't Nita have a boyfriend?

Steve:

She can have as many boyfriends as her heart desires, as long as she don't mind me cutting their little wee-wees off.

Steve and Miguel laugh, while Anita whines to Sonrisa, who chides her husband.

Anita:

Mama, make them stop.

Sonrisa:

(to Anita) Steve is just teasing you, nina. (to Steve) Leave her alone.

Steve:

It ain't her I'm worried about. (to Miguel) You, on the other hand, better have as many girlfriends as you can carry. (to Anita) Don't get some mother's son hurt. (He winks at Sonrisa, who smiles at Anita, as Miguel laughs.) (to Anita) As a matter of fact, call the convent, tell them we have a new recruit coming.

Everyone but Anita laughs, as she pouts and folds her arms.

Crossfade to Steve spooning with Sonrisa in their bed, talking about the day's events, as Wisin Y Yandel-Besos Mejados plays throughout.

Sonrisa:

Mi Diablito, I have some good news.

Steve:

Mi angelita, I have some bad news.

Sonrisa:

Then, you better go first.

Steve:

That blood you found on me belonged to Chico and Carlos. Long story short, I killed them in the back of that limo.

Sonrisa turns to face him, horrified.

Sonrisa:

Why, mi marido, why?!

Steve:

Because, the man is so damn arrogant. And, knowing what he did to you does not help his case at all, especially when he thinks it's so damn cute, throwing it in our faces. He had the audacity to say that we disrespected him by not inviting him to the wedding and Quinceañera.

Sonrisa:

What made you kill Carlos and Chico?

Steve:

First, he asked the dumbest question I've ever heard. He asked why we didn't invite him to the events. I told him, quite rudely, just why. One thing led to another, before I knew it, the war of words, became an all-out war. And, he pissed himself.

Sonrisa:

( laughing) No, he didn't. Coward! How could you, Mi Diablito?

Steve:

Because, I think I've finally figured out why I'm here. Just as I still can't explain just what is behind the force that brought us together, all I know is that, me and you were meant to be. I've never felt a hatred this intense, or a need to cause someone as much pain and suffering as possible, as I do when Vibora opens his mouth, especially when he disrespects you. When he says something derogatory about you, I can actually feel my blood boil. So, I think I'm here, not only to bring you and I the experience of true love and happiness, I'm also here to avenge the innocence that he stole from you, and bring grief to someone that has probably never known true pain, only gave it out.

Sonrisa:

(wiping tears away) Mi conquistadorito, I love you, so much, mi amor.

Steve:

I should hope so; I just started a war with a drug lord over you. (He smiles at her.)

Sonrisa:

Tell me you love me, mi amor.

Steve:

I love you, Mrs. Davis.

She snuggles into him.

Sonrisa:

I like that, Mrs. Davis. Now, for my news.

Steve:

Yes, the good news. Brighten my day, angelita.

Sonrisa:

(She looks into his eyes and places his right hand on her stomach.) I'm pregnant, mi amor.

Steve stares blankly into her eyes. She moderately panics and kisses him.

Sonrisa:

Mi Diablito, I wanted you to be happy.

( trying enthusiastically to calm her nerves) No, baby, no. I'm extremely happy. (He pulls her closer to him and kisses her cheek.) I guess I'm still not over losing my last baby, and I don't want to lose this one.

Now it's her turn to do the reassuring, hitting him with a barrage of facial kisses.

Sonrisa:

Mi amor, please don't say such things, or even think them. Our baby's going to be so beautiful and healthy and precious. Tell me you believe me. (She places his hand on her stomach.)

Steve:

I believe you, angelita.

Sonrisa:

Swear to me as you hold our child.

Steve:

( rubbing her stomach) I swear I believe you.

Outside the door, Anita and Miguel eavesdrop.

Miguel:

They're going to love the baby they made together more than all of us combined.

Anita:

( hitting his arm) Shut up, Miggy, and listen.

In the bedroom, Steve and Sonrisa separate from a deep kiss.

Steve:

And, do you know what the best part is?

Sonrisa:

What's that, mi amor?

Steve:

It'll be born into a family that's bound together, not only by love, but trust.

A split-screen reveals Anita and Miguel, listening.

Sonrisa:

Tell me what you mean.

Steve:

Who knows how long Nita and Miggy were wandering around by themselves, living off of trash before you found them? Or just how many people passed them by and left them to fend for themselves? But, the moment you chose to take them in, they loved you, because they knew that they could trust you. Now, they know that, I love you, knowing you had them. I came, introduced myself, and married you. And, all I can do is hope that, if they don't love me, that they can at least trust me. So, our baby will be born in one strong family that knows what it's like to not only have been abandoned, but also to be rescued. That means we'll never abandon each other, knowing what it entails. Me, you, Nita, and Miggy were all abandoned, and all of us were rescued by one another. You rescued them, and you and I rescued each other. And, here we are.

Sonrisa:

(crying) Come to me, papi.

She lies on her back, spreading her legs, and Steve licks her clitoris a few times.

Sonrisa:

Come to me, now, papi!

He obeys, and she greets him with a kiss and wraps her arms around his neck. He smiles down on her, wiping her tears away.

Steve:

So full of tears, mamacita.

Sonrisa:

And. Now…

He enters her gently.

Sonrisa:

( gasping in ecstasy) I'm so full of you.

Love is made. Anita and Miguel giggle as they listen.

Anita:

No wonder they made that baby.

Miguel:

Right?! That's all they do.

Act 6-Scene 18-1:17 A.M.; Pitbull-Defense plays as a livid Vibora continues his rant to Renaldo, Blake, Henry, Aaron, and Jesus about...

Vibora:

...That goddamn American nigger actually put a gun in my face!!!

He slams his fist onto his desk.

Henry:

Patron, we know all of this, do you want us to go at him full speed, or cruise control?

Vibora:

There's no need to go at him full speed. It's just him, his whore wife, and three bastards. We own the police, not all, but the most important ones. He may have married a Colombiana, but, he's still a stranger, and this isn't his land. The only thing is that, he's a killer, and he doesn't fear or respect me.

He is going to shoot first and ask no questions. So, first, we'll try to start slow, and, if that fails, we'll turn it up.

Meanwhile: 1:43 A.M.: At Freddie's bar, he and Steve sit in his office as Ilegales-Ayantame plays.

Freddie:

So, the wife's pregnant, and you've started a war with the most powerful Drug Lord in Colombia? (He chuckles as he pours them both a shot of gin.)

Steve downs his drink.

Freddie:

( sarcastically) Congratulations, I guess?

Steve:

Asshole.

They both laugh.

Steve:

I know we just met a few months ago, but, I can't go at this alone. It's impossible. Can I call on you if I need you?

Freddie:

Your timing is impeccable. This bastard knows that I don't like pimping women and sex-trafficking, so, he comes in earlier and tells me he's going to be commandeering my club, for those very purposes.

Steve:

Sounds like a yes to me.

Freddie:

You guessed it.

Steve:

Let me ask you something.

Freddie:

Shoot.

Steve:

Why you all haven't been started something with this cat?

Freddie:

It's hard when he basically runs everything. Plus, I don't know what it is, but, I feel a confidence that was never there before when I hear you speak of going to war with him.

Steve:

Plus, you've never really been a gunslinger, you've always tried to steer clear?

Freddie:

I've tried, but, it's virtually impossible to duck bullshit in Colombia.

Steve:

Tell me about it. The biggest drug lord in Colombia started fucking with me the first week I got here, all over a girl that he took everything from and supposedly cares nothing about. Go figure. Not to mention, the man pissed his pants when I shot his boys and put the gun in his face.

Freddie smiles.

Freddie:

Are you serious?!

Steve:

Dead serious. Deep down, the man ain't tough at all. I've shot and been shot at, by some truly tough guys. He's living off of his father's reputation. Won't be the first time that's ever been done, most definitely won't be the last. Not saying he won't kill, just saying that, deep down, he's not tough. I discovered his weakness.

Freddie:

Which is?

Steve:

He's never been challenged.

Meanwhile: 2:21 A.M.: Anita and Miguel watch television in their living talking the night away.

Anita:

Why do you call Steve papa?

Miguel:

Because.

Anita:

Because what, stupid? (She pushes his head.)

Miguel:

Because he's here, stupid.

Anita:

For now.

Miguel:

For good.

Anita:

How do you know?

Miguel:

When we listen outside their bedroom door, can't you hear the way that they talk to each other?

Anita:

I still wake up in the middle of the night, waiting for him to come in and…

She stops abruptly, as images of her being raped flash into her mind. Miguel

157

scoots closer to her, placing his arm around her shoulder.

Miguel:

Hermana, he's been here since his birthday, three months ago. He married Mama on your birthday, threw you a Quinceañera, remodeled our house, and has just killed two men over Mama. If he was going to do something to you, he'd've done it already. All of the other guys never took any interest in us, at all. Never gave us anything. Never cared about us or Mama, outside of sex.

Anita:

And, I've never seen mamita this happy. Ever! He's American, he could've went back to America, a far better place than this, if he was going to leave.

Miguel:

But he's still here.

Miguel places a pillow on her lap and lays his head on it. Anita leans back and they both ease off into a deep sleep. A time lapse brightens the scene into morning.

Scene 19-8:27 A.M.: Sonrisa, Steve, and Marcos stare at Miguel and Anita asleep on the couch, in the same position they drifted off in. Sonrisa grabs her phone from the coffee table, aims at the slumbering pair, and snaps a photo, cooing at Steve.

Sonrisa:

Look at our kids, mi amor. After all of their fighting.

Steve:

Brother and sister.

The scene fades into them, all dressed in royal blue in the living room, prepping for their family picture, as a female photographer does some last minute fidgeting. Sonrisa sits on Steve's left thigh, holding Marcos, while Anita stands behind Steve's right shoulder, and Miguel stands behind Sonrisa.

The photographer walks to her camera that's posted on a tripod, makes a few focusing adjustments as she peers at the family of five, and says…

Photographer:

Okay, everybody, smile.

They obey, and three seconds later, the camera's click, materializes the image into a picture, which looms into a painting, that ends up on the wall, over the couch, with the photograph in the bottom left corner of the painting's frame as the family admires it.

It's now one month later, September.

Sonrisa:

I love it, it's beautiful.

Steve:

Yeah, I agree.

Miguel:

I'm hungry.

Anita:

Me, too.

Gunshots are heard as bullets fly through the living room window, causing everyone to—

Steve:

GET THE FUCK DOWN!!!

Sonrisa covers the kids, as Steve covers her, and points to the hallway

Steve:

GO, GO, GO, GO, GO, DOWN THE HALL!!!

Everyone makes their way to the hallway as bullets continue to fly through the windows, breaking various household items, but never hitting the painting.

The gunshots stop, and Steve pulls his .9mm from his spine.

Steve:

Stay right here, and don't move!

He runs to the window and hears car doors opening, then closing. Three doors slam shut. He peeks through the drapes and sees three individuals, teenagers, all brandishing assault rifles. He walks to the side of the door, and holds his gun straight out, aiming.

The men can barely be heard as they mumble outside the door, and Steve looks back at his family, putting his finger to his lips, signaling for silence. The door flies open, and two men rush into gunfire. Both men take multiple face and headshots, which takes the third gunman by surprise. Steve is very still, studying the shadow of the third assailant-

Steve:

(yelling at the gunman) Whatcha gon' do, amigo?! I ain't got all day. From the looks of your partners AK and AR-15, you're decent with your weapon, so, shoot or walk off.

Steve backpedals away from the door, never taking his eyes off of it, that is, until he hears what must be the driver's door closing. He takes a quick look through the curtain, affirming his assumption, as the driver looks in either direction, holding a handgun down with both hands, using his head to gesture his comrade toward the door.

Steve points the gun at the first man, and fires, hitting him three times in the chest, as the other three shots stray, leaving the slide in the empty position. The driver sees this, and retreats to the car, speeding away loudly.

Steve motions to his family that everything is clear. They come toward him slowly, Sonrisa carrying a crying Marcos, who reaches for Steve. Steve takes him and tries in vain to calm him.

Steve:

Shhh, papi. It's okay, now, hijo. It's okay.

He kisses his cheek, and Marcos lays his head on Steve's shoulder, crying softly now, calming somewhat.

Steve:

When the police get here…

Sonrisa:

If Vibora sent these men, you don't have to worry about the police coming.

Steve:

I almost forgot. Colombia, home of the corrupt.

Steve removes his cellular phone from his right pocket, presses one button, and, after two rings, Freddie picks up.

A split-screen reveals Freddie performing cunnilingus on a lady who sits on his desk, using her two fingers to spread her clit, for easier access.

Freddie:

(annoyed) What do you want, Steven?!

Steve:

I need a garbage truck.

Freddie:

What?!

Steve:

You heard me. The Boss sent his men, and they failed.

Freddie:

Perfect timing, amigo.

Steve:

Get your head out of that stripper's lap and let's do this.

Anita's eyes bulge and her mouth drops in shock as she grabs Sonrisa's arm. Miguel asks...

Miguel:

What would Freddie's head be doing in a stripper's lap?

Sonrisa:

(placing her hand over Miguel's mouth) Shh, hijo.

She reprimands Steve by lightly punching his arm.

Steve:

You say you and your brothers have plenty guns, right?

Freddie:

This is Cali, Colombia. The priests have guns here, hermano.

Steve:

Amen. I also have a plan.

Grupo Mania-A Que Te Pego Mi Mania plays throughout the montage.

Show the driver of the gunmen's car in a split-screen talking to Vibora as he weaves through traffic at a moderately high speed.

Driver:

He got lucky, boss!

Vibora:

I'm not trying to hear that bullshit!!! You fucks had numbers and assault rifles, he's one man with a handgun, a whore, and three bastards!!!

Driver:

I'll get more men, Vibora!

Vibora slams the receiver onto its base.

Show Steve, Freddie, and Johnny in a field, tossing the three dead men into a grave, dousing their bodies with gasoline, and Freddie lighting one match, using it to light the rest of the book, and tossing it onto the pile of dead men, which goes up in flames.

Show the eight ladies all gathered on a porch, across from Sonrisa's house, five houses to the right, discussing Steve.

Bethany:

Oh, my God, chicas. I wish a man would start a war over me.

Rosalita:

Makes me so wet just thinking about it.

Penelope:

Muchachas, when I saw Steve come out holding that gun, then he took Marcos from Sonrisa, I had to stop myself from raping him in front of everyone.

They collectively cackle.

Ilanny:

I want some of those orgasms he's giving Sonrisa, with that big black dick.

They all laugh.

Show Steve entering Miguel and Marcos' room with a black .9mm in his right hand, Miguel tosses his iPad to the side and perks up as Steve sits next to him.

Steve:

Hijo, I need you to pay attention. Your mother doesn't know about this.

Miguel:

Okay.

Steve pulls the clip from the handle, then yanks the slide back, ejecting the bullet from the chamber, catching it with his left hand, to Miguel's delight. Steve smiles at him, and begins his lesson.

Steve:

See how the slide stays back? (He holds the chamber up to his eye, peering at Miguel through the handle.) It does that whenever you empty the clip. (He puts the gun between he and Miguel, then places the loose bullet into the clip, slamming the clip into the handle, causing the slide to move forward.) Now it's ready to shoot. Every time you shoot the clip empty, and the slide locks back, when you put a new loaded clip in, the slide goes forward and puts a bullet in the chamber as it does that. Whenever you empty the clip, this button (showing Miguel the safety) goes up, holding the slide back. So, if it's empty, and you pull the safety down, the slide goes forward with no bullets. If you put the clip in, you'll have to pull the slide back to put a bullet in the chamber. And, whenever you pull the slide back to put a bullet in the chamber, and remove the clip, the gun will shoot, because you leave the bullet in the chamber, even though you remove the clip.

Miguel:

So, when it's empty and the slide locks back, when you put a clip in, it loads automatically. If it's empty and you push the slide forward while it's empty, if you put a fresh clip in, you'll have to pull the slide back in order to put one in the chamber.

Steve:

There it is.

Miguel:

Can I shoot it, now?!

Steve:

Hell no!

Miguel:

Why not?!

Steve:

Are you trying to shoot someone in this house?

Miguel:

No.

Steve:

Okay, then. I just want you to know what you're doing if and when the time comes. I don't need you finding this and accidentally killing one of us. And, only when we're under attack, will I give you this. When I do, you squeeze this as tightly as you can with both hands, aim low, like at their stomachs, because the kick from the gun will make your shot rise, and, you'll more than likely hit them in the chest, hopefully their heads. And, whenever you're not using, or intending to use this (showing him the safety and pushing it up, locking the slide into place), make sure this button is always up. Because if you don't, and you slip up and shoot somebody in this house, by mistake, you know what I'm going to do, don't you?

Miguel nods in the negative with his eyes bulging. Steve pulls out a giant seven-inch, jagged edged knife with his right hand, and grabs Miguel's shirt, pulling him toward him, tickling him.

Steve:

I'ma cut ya wee-wee off!

They laugh, while Sonrisa looks in on them, smiling to herself.

Show Steve, along with Freddie and his four brothers, drinking in Freddie's closed club, the time is 3:51 A.M., while Angel Y Khriz-La Apuesta plays.

Steve:

My family is vulnerable right now. What's up, fellas?

Freddie:

It looks as if you have some more guerillas on your side, amigo. Vibora knows that I don't want to have anything to do with pimping or sex-trafficking, but, he thinks my brothers and I won't fight him. It's bad enough I got a strip club, but, at least these ladies want to be here voluntarily. This is where I draw the line.

Raul:

I got the guns, grenades, and more, hermanos.

Johnny:

And, I know about his next outgoing shipment.

Steve:

That's what I like to do, fuck with his pockets!

Costas:

We'll figure something out, very soon.

Franco:

It has to be soon. Everybody's talking about the Black American who started a war with Vibora over a girl he forced to be a whore. (He rubs Steve's bald head.) You've made you and you lady legends, hermano. No one has ever stood against Don Jefe.

Freddie:

You're famous.

Steve:

Since I'm so famous, where's my fortune?

Everyone laughs and downs shots. Fade into the next scene.

Scene 20-9:43 A.M.: The Next Day.

Sonrisa stares out of their living room window at Anita, who is currently in her pajamas, talking to her boyfriend, Paulo, when Steve wraps his arms around her waist from behind, pulling her to him. She tilts her head to the left, closing her eyes, moaning as he kisses her neck.

Steve:

Good Morning, querida.

Sonrisa:

Good Morning, mi marido.

Steve:

Whatcha doing, bird watching?

Sonrisa:

You could say that.

Steve looks out and sees Anita and Paulo, sharing that nervous smile teenage couples share right before they—

Steve:

—Kiss!

Sonrisa:

Isn't it sweet? I think this will be her first kiss. I'm so excited for her.

Steve:

I don't know about all of this kissing. It's only nine-something in the morning.

Sonrisa:

(She giggles while turning to face him, putting her arms around his neck, kissing him.) You just kissed me, and, we do more than kiss earlier than this.

Steve:

I know that. But, we're married, plus, my name is Steve, I do what I want.

He kisses her and walks speedily down the hall to their bedroom and Sonrisa looks out of the window at the teenage couple, now holding hands. Steve comes back into the room putting something down his spine, causing Sonrisa's eyes to bulge.

Sonrisa:

Diablo, what're you doing?!

Steve:

About to go scare the shit out of the young man we can't eat dinner without hearing his name. (He scowls, feigning disgust, saying the name with a scoff.) Paulo, he looks like a damn Paulo.

Sonrisa:

And how do all Paulos look?

Steve:

Like horny-ass teenagers who want to stick their slimy ass body parts in and out of my babygirl.

Sonrisa smiles at him and turns toward the window, just as Anita steps closer to Paulo. Steve looks just in time, kissing Sonrisa's cheek.

Steve:

That's my cue.

Sonrisa:

(swatting his arm as he exits) Mi Diablito!

Anita and Paulo jump, startled back to reality at the sound of…

Steve:

Good Morning, lovers. Don't stop on my account!

Anita:

(She blushes, clearly embarrassed, and drops her head.) Oh, my God! (to Paulo) Stay!

Paulo stares nervously at Steve, but stands his ground as Steve approaches and Anita takes a few steps toward him, placing her hands on his chest.

Anita:

Steve, leave him alone!

Steve:

I just want to meet the man who seems to interrupt all of our dinner conversations.

Steve extends his right hand, which holds his .9mm, causing Paulo to attempt to flee.

Paulo:

(to Anita) I'm about to go, 'Nita…

Steve:

Who gave you permission to leave? You must've wanted something, coming over here at 9 A.M. And, I know exactly what you wanted, too.

Anita:

(dropping her head into her hands) Oh, my God!

Steve:

(to Paulo) You know who I am, don't you? (He reaches for something that is strapped to his waist, while putting his gun away.)

Paulo:

Everybody knows who the black American is.

Steve pulls out the seven-inch jagged-edged buck knife, looking at Anita.

Steve:

Remember what I told you I was gon' do to your boyfriends?

Anita:

Oh, my God.

Steve:

(to Paulo) Pull your dick out.

Paulo:

(eyes wide) What?! (looking at Anita) Who exactly is he to you?

Steve:

You talk to me, I'm talking to you. I'm her father.

Paulo:

You're black!

Steve:

(feigning anger, waving the knife by Paulo's midsection) That's it, pull your dick out, you lil' racist bastard! A black man can't be her father?!

Anita:

He meant—

Steve:

I know exactly what he meant! (to Paulo) And, you, you're a Mexican, right?!

Paulo:

I'm Colombian!

Steve:

That's what they all say. I'm sorry, you all look alike to me. See how that feels?

Anita:

Oh, my God, Steve!

Steve:

(to Anita) Okay, 'Nita. Just let me have a quick word with Paulo, here?! (He turns to Anita and winks at her, she, in turn, calms a bit as she watches them step out of earshot.)

Once he and Paulo are a few feet away, Steve begins his brief rationalization.

Steve:

(He extends his right hand to Paulo for a shake, which Paulo does.) Paulo, I did that for a reason. Don't look at her, look at me. Now, here's what's going to happen. I don't know exactly how much about Anita's past you're familiar with or even if this is you two's first kiss (Paulo nods in the affirmative), so, when you two kiss, do not, I REPEAT, DO NOT put your hands up her shirt, and most definitely don't reach down her pants, my wife is watching, that's her mother. If you put your hands down her pants while my wife is watching, I'm putting this knife down yours. (He briefly waves the knife in Paulo's face.) I'm saying this reluctantly, but, I'll allow a butt squeeze, you two are fifteen, I mean, I'm not a monster. I'm a man, too. I've been there. Plus, they like that. So, wait here.

Steve walks to Anita  and hugs her, kissing her forehead.

Sonrisa smiles and wipes a tear from her cheek, saying to herself…

Sonrisa:

Mi Diablito.

Outside, Steve tells Anita…

Steve:

Have fun, mi amor.

Anita:

Why did you torture him?

Steve:

That's what all fathers do to their daughters' boyfriends. It lets them know that you have a protector. Plus, it's just fun.

She smiles and swats his chest.

Steve:

And, I wanted you to have the experience of having your father make your boyfriend uncomfortable.

They exchange smiles and she hugs him. He kisses her forehead.

Steve:

Have fun, Nita.

Steve enters the house and is immediately greeted with Sonrisa's tongue in his mouth as J-Alvarez-La Pregunta begins to play softly.

Steve:

What was that for?

Sonrisa:

Mi Diablito, it was because I love you, and I know exactly why you did what you just did.

Steve:

I think you may be missing your daughter's—

Sonrisa:

—OUR daughter's…

Steve:

—excuse me, our daughter's first kiss.

They take the necessary step to the window and look out at the teenage lovers. The song plays loudly as Anita and Paulo share their first kiss.

Steve:

I can't watch this.

Sonrisa:

Shhh, mi amor. You made this happen. That was so sweet of you. Look…

Outside, Paulo squeezes Anita's behind and Sonrisa squeals.

Steve:

I'm 'bout to go cut his balls off.

Sonrisa wraps her arm around his head and kisses his cheek.

Sonrisa:

Mi enamorado, I love you. We need those for our grandchildren.

Steve:

I love you, too.

Miguel and Marcos stumble in behind them.

Miguel:

Who's outside?

Steve:

Your sister's kissing her boyfriend.

Miguel:

There goes breakfast.

Steve:

That's why you shouldn't ask so many questions, you get answers.

Miguel:

You could've just said Anita and her boyfriend.

Steve:

Go get Marcos some cereal. (to Sonrisa) Come on, baby. You've seen enough.

Sonrisa:

(reluctantly turning to Steve) I'm so jealous. I want a kiss from mi esposo.

She wraps her arms around his neck and they kiss.

Miguel:

(exhaling heavily so that they can hear him) Haven't you two kissed enough this morning? We're trying to eat in here.

They ignore him.

Anita and Paulo separate, oblivious to the fact that, there's a black van parked down the street, with Jesus in the driver's seat, Aaron in the passenger's seat, and Renaldo, Blake, and Henry in the rear.

Blake:

Isn't that sweet?

Jesus:

It sure is.

Anita tells Paulo…

Anita:

I have to go, mi amor.

Paulo:

Can I come by later?

Anita:

Okay.

Paulo:

Tell your father, that, if he needs my help with Vibora—

Anita:

—No, mi amor, I don't want you to get hurt.

Paulo:

I don't want to get hurt either. But, I'm falling in love with his daughter.

They smile and kiss quickly.

Paulo:

And, he can't be the only man protecting you and your family, which, by extension, is my family. You'll tell him?

She pecks his lips and walks toward the door.

Anita:

Yes, I'll see what he says.

They exchange one last goodbye peck, and part ways.

Inside, Steve feeds Marcos and speaks into his cell phone. A split-screen reveals Freddie.

Freddie:

I know you don't want to leave your family, hermano, but, you started this war, so you have to fight it. We're going to drop off some weapons for you. But right now, in a few hours, Vibora's shipment is going out, and, we need our leader badly, so—

Steve:

—I get it. What time will you be arriving?

Freddie:

Around two.

Steve:

Adios.

They disconnect just as Anita takes a seat next to Sonrisa, swooning. They both squeal and hold hands.

Anita:

He said he's falling in love with me.

She and Sonrisa giggle and touch foreheads as Steve and Miguel roll their eyes. Sonrisa notices this.

Sonrisa:

You two better not ruin this moment for us, I mean her.

Steve:

No, you had it right the first time. I just would like to say that, in light of this joyous occasion, that I told quite a few women the same thing when I was trying to do stuff to them.

Sonrisa:

Diablo!

Miguel laughs as Anita and Sonrisa shoot Steve evil-eyes.

Steve:

(placing his left hand on Anita's shoulder, saying in a voice heavily laden with sarcasm) But, mi amor, I'm sure you've managed to find true love in your first kiss. You ain't the first teenage girl to get that lucky, and trust me, you won't be the last. Your mother wants grandbabies already, won't let me cut his balls off.

Anita folds her arms and pouts angrily as Sonrisa comforts her, and Miguel laughs along with Steve.

Anita:

Do you think it's funny that he said he'd help you with Vibora?

Sonrisa:

Awww, that's—

Steve:

—Not gon' happen.

Anita:

Why not? He said you shouldn't be the only man protecting this family.

Sonrisa:

Awww!

Steve:

Angelita, stop that! (to Anita) Listen, I'm not about to have some boy's blood on me, physically or mentally. Second of all, we don't really know him. He could be sex-trafficker for all we know. I know you just had your first kiss, he told you that he almost loves you. I know how you're feeling, but, this is grown man business, here. If he comes up paralyzed, or dead, I refuse to have you or my wife, blaming me for it. You two just have fun with your relationship. Enjoy each other before you send him off to war.

Sonrisa:

(placing her hand on Anita's shoulder in a vain attempt to comfort her) He's right, mi amor, you'd never forgive yourself if something happened to him.

Anita:

( standing, raising her voice slightly) I would be able to because he'd be fighting for me. You already know what that feels like, Steve started a war over you! (to Steve) And, what if it was Mama?!

Steve:

I knew that was coming. 'Nita, I hate to compare you two's past experiences, but, luckily, for you, Sonrisa found you just in time to spare you the horrors she went through. But, to answer your question, honestly, nothing would stop me from fighting for her. Luckily, I started this war, so, nothing can stop me. I do appreciate the gallantry in his gesture, but, if Vibora finds out that you two are together, he may try to hurt him, by hurting you, which would hurt us all. And, I most definitely have to protect you. Keeping Paulo from getting too involved in this is just another way that I have to do that.

Anita storms off.

Sonrisa takes Anita's seat to be closer to Steve.

Sonrisa:

She's never been that mad before, papi.

Steve:

She's fifteen. You two never argue?

Sonrisa:

Yes, but she's never—

Steve:

—had a boyfriend involved in the argument. Seems as if I brought excitement your lives. (He winks and grins at Sonrisa.) You're welcome.

Sonrisa:

Diablo!

Miguel playfully slaps the table, stands, feigning anger, folds his arms.

Miguel:

I'm mad, too!

Marcos slaps the table, laughing as Steve and Sonrisa look at Miguel askance.

Sonrisa:

Why are you mad, mi nino?

Miguel:

I don't know!

He storms off and can be heard laughing as he exits.

There's a knock at the door. Steve grabs his .9mm from his waist and yells.

Steve:

Who is it?

Freddie:

Freddie and Raul.

Steve checks the peephole, and opens the door upon confirmation. Freddie and Raul both carry two giant duffel bags, which are clearly heavy, as they rush in and drop them with a clang.

Freddie:

Change in plans, mi amigo, we have to go now!

Steve:

It's always something.

Sonrisa:

Where're you going, and what am I supposed to do with all of these guns?

Steve:

I think the less you know about what we're about to do, the better. And, do you know how to use assault rifles?

Sonrisa:

You'd be surprised the things you learn growing up in a brothel.

Steve:

Well, first of all, I wouldn't. Put them under the bed, away from Miggy, as a matter of fact ( looking at Freddie and Raul as he picks up two of the bags), fellas, if you'd grab those and follow me, please?

They do, and briskly make their way to the bedroom and back in four or five seconds.

Raul:

I like the bullet holes, heh, gives the place that true, Colombian touch.

They all share a tense laugh as Sonrisa makes her way to Steve, putting her arms around his neck.

Sonrisa:

Baby, be careful, whatever you're about to do.

They peck lips a few times as Marcos walks up, reaching for Steve, who lifts him, kissing his cheek.

Steve:

I'll be back in a few, papito.

Marcos kisses Steve's cheek and pulls his head to him, hugging him, causing Sonrisa to coo at them, Steve hands Marcos to his mother and looks at Freddie

Steve:

Ready, Freddie?

Freddie:

Si.

Act 7-Scene 21: Calle 13-La Madre De La Enanos begins as the five gentlemen in the van watch Steve, Freddie, and Raul enter a pick-up truck. Blake holds a knife to Paulo's throat, saying...

Blake:

We'll see if you still like that bitch once we're through with her!

The five bandits laugh as Paulo squirms in anger, vainly attempting to free himself.

Meanwhile: Johnny, Costas, Franco, and two of their cousins, Ferdinand and Jorge, watch from a hill as many men pack the cabs of two 18-wheelers with kilos of cocaine.

Ferdinand:

Did everyone bring their straws?

Everybody laughs as Steve, Raul, and Freddie pull up and immediately blend into both the crowd and the conversation.

Jorge:

Steve, have you ever seen that much coke in your life?

Steve:

Not at all.

Franco:

What're we going to do with all of it?

Steve:

Burn it.

The crowd, with the expostulation of Steve, collectively disagrees with a chorus of shock.

Johnny:

Mi hermano, do you know how much money that is?!

No. But, I do know this, this is war. And when we take it, if we get away with it, Vibora has the police in his pocket, we won't be able to hide it, let alone sell it. Not to mention the fact that we'll have to keep killing anyway, because everyone knows I'm behind it. So, the best thing we can do with all of this shit is send him a message, by wasting it.

Raul:

You're the first American I ever met who wanted to willingly burn cocaine without smoking it.

Steve:

It's nice to meet you, too, mi hermano.

All laugh.

Meanwhile: Sonrisa washes dishes as Marcos plays in the water next to her, when the front door is kicked in. She turns in horror upon seeing the five men, one holding a knife to Paulo's throat-

Jesus:

(barking to his crowd) Go get the other two!

Jesus pulls a .357 Magnum from his waist and aims it at Sonrisa.

Jesus:

You know the drill.

He walks to her as she brazenly stares him down. As soon as he is close enough, she slaps him and spits in his face. He wipes it clean.

Jesus:

You can thank your nigger husband for this.

The three men return, Renaldo dragging a kicking and screaming Anita, and Aaron holding a stone-faced Miguel by his right arm.

Paulo:

Leave them alone, you cowards!!!

Blake:

( pressing the knife against his neck, causing a stream of blood to crawl slowly down his neck) Shut up, dog!!!

Renaldo drags Anita to the table, where her mother is already bent over, pleading.

Sonrisa:

(Earnestly, crying) Please leave her alone, her and my sons?!!! Please?!!! Do whatever you want to me, just leave her and my sons alone?!!!

Jesus:

Now, why would we only fuck one old whore, when there's a younger, tighter, fresher whore of her daughter right here?!

He and Renaldo simultaneously snatch the ladies bottoms down as they both cry out, Sonrisa to Miguel and Paulo.

Sonrisa:

Don't look, boys, don't look! Close your eyes, just close your eyes!

Aaron pulls a .45 from his waist and points it at Miguel's head as he cries and struggles. Blake pulls Paulo's head up.

Aaron:

(softly into Miguel's ear) If you look away, I'll kill you, nino! Do you think I'm joking?

Miguel nods 'no.'

Blake:

I'll cut your fucking head clean off of your shoulders if you look away!

Paulo:

You fucking cowards!!! Bastards!!!

Blake:

(laughing devilishly into his ear) We saw you two kiss, today, so, you know who I'm going to fuck! Hope you don't mind.

Jesus and Renaldo penetrate both ladies anuses in sync, causing them to wince in pain, as they clinch in vain.

Meanwhile: Steve and his gang of seven make their way to their respective vehicles as they see men closing the cabs of the 18-wheelers, and slapping the sides, signaling to the driver.

Jorge:

Let's move!

Meanwhile: Jesus pulls Sonrisa's hair back, causing her to lift her head with tears streaming down her face.

Jesus:

Look right at your son, bitch, or we will kill the baby first!

She looks at Miguel reluctantly, saying to herself...

Sonrisa:

Don't look, hijo, don't look.

Renaldo:

(to Anita, as he pulls her hair back) The same goes for you, puta, look right at your boyfriend.

She does, and vomits.

Meanwhile: Freddie drives the truck, while Steve sits in the cab, holding a chrome AK-47 on his lap. Raul occupies the passenger seat, nursing an M-16.

Johnny, Costas, and Franco occupy a similar pick-up truck, with Costas in the cab with an AR-fifteen, and Franco in the passenger seat with an AK-47.

Ferdinand drives the pick-up, while his brother Jorge sits in the passenger seat, nursing an M-16. Jorge looks at two loaded rocket launchers in the backseat.

Arcangel-Me Prefieres A Mi plays throughout the scene as Jorge sticks his upper body out of the window, and opens fire at the right rear tire of the 18-wheeler that's in front of them. He blows a tire out, but is alerted by shots from behind him as two bullets whiz by his head.

Nine automobiles distinguish themselves from the others on the road, as their respective passengers all stick their frames out, and start shooting.

Costas and Steve both send cover fire. The lead 18-wheeler takes the next right. Jorge notices, along with Johnny, who takes Jorge's signal and turns right as four security vehicles follow them. The closest 18-wheeler, with the blown right rear tire, takes a left, with Freddie and Ferdinand following, and the remaining five security cars are closely in tow.

Going right, Costas aims at the car on his left, and fires, the first few shots drift, while three find the shooting passenger's head, knocking chunks from his forehead, face, and neck, killing him instantly, as he releases his weapon, and his corpse dangles from the window. Costas now aims carefully, but ducks immediately upon being fired on. A few bullets hit the cab, and Franco slides the back window open, sticking his gun out, and aims to the right, sending cover fire, striking the windshield, causing a red splatter to appear on it as the driver is hit, causing the car to swerve right, crushing the passenger between another car, sending them both into other cars, causing a severe pile-up, followed by an explosion, leaving two cars in pursuit.

Meanwhile: Jesus and Renaldo hold the ladies heads down as they tuck their penises into their underwear, and wait for Blake and Aaron to come and to their places behind the women, they take their cohorts places holding Paulo and Miguel hostage, as Marcos cries on the floor.

Sonrisa:

Please, just cover my baby's eyes?! Please!

Aaron:

Don't worry about that now, whore!

He penetrates her anus, causing her to lower her head. Blake stares at Paulo as he frees his erection from his pants.

Blake:

Hope you enjoy her after I'm through with her. (He smiles menacingly at Paulo, then enters Anita's anal cavity, causing her to resume her crying.)

Meanwhile: Steve and Raul both fire at the five cars that are in hot pursuit of them, as Jorge hoists a rocket launcher onto his right shoulder as best as he can at this speed, Ferdinand hits a pothole, causing Jorge to almost drop the weapon, which he manages to hold onto just before losing it. He readjusts, but, not before cursing his brother and slapping the roof.

Jorge:

Hermano, be careful, asshole!

Ferdinand:

Shut up, and shoot, already!

Steve and Raul make contact with two of the vehicles, Raul blowing the front left tire of a vehicle on his left, causing him to spin out and into another car, and Steve hits a gunman in the chest, making him fall backward and out of his vehicle, only to be run over by the car behind him as Steve also paints the windshield red, making contact with the driver's face.

Jorge fires the rocket launcher, and tosses it as the rocket makes contact, exploding the entire cab, sending burning and open kilos raining down as the entire truck goes up in flames. Steve takes a bullet in and out of his left shoulder as Freddie swerves left to avoid the flaming truck, and Ferdinand goes right, to do the same. The cars that were in pursuit stop following, as what they were hired to secure, is now up in smoke.

Meanwhile: Blake and Aaron laugh maniacally as they finish with the ladies, leaving them crying and slumping to the floor, as Sonrisa cries, pulling a crying Marcos to her with her right hand, and Anita scoots into her embrace on her left side. Jesus and Renaldo releases Paulo and Miguel, who sit, frozen.

Jesus:

Tell the nigger Vibora says hello.

All five men laugh at this as they leave, Miguel and Paulo don't move until the men are completely out of the house. Miguel runs to Sonrisa, as Paulo approaches Anita, but is met with a violent resistance as she kicks and screams at him to…

Anita:

Paulo, get away from me!!! Please?!!! Please leave now?!!!

Paulo:

But, mi amor…

Anita:

( bursting into a fresh fit of tears and leaning into Sonrisa) Gooooooooo!!!!

Sonrisa:

Give her a few days, Paulo. She's so ashamed, right now.

Paulo looks down on the crying Anita, sharing shame, as he was powerless to help her, and reluctantly leaves the family to comfort each other.

RKM Y Ken-Y Forever plays as Sonrisa holds Anita to her as they both sit in the tub, letting the shower rain down on them as they share tears, while Miguel sits outside the bathroom door, rocking a sleeping Marcos. Anita asks Sonrisa, through tears…

Anita:

Is this it for me? Am I going to get raped my entire life?

Sonrisa:

(crying harder as she squeezes Anita tighter to her, trying desperately to comfort her) No, nina, no. Don't ever say that, mi amor. (She kisses her forehead.) Those men are animals. One day you'll find your true love, and he'll make you forget all about those monsters who violated you, hija. And when you do, it'll be beautiful. Trust me.

Anita:

Like Steve did with you?

Sonrisa:

Yes, mi amor. Just like that. Thinking of Steve is helping me right now.

Meanwhile: Freddie and Ferdinand speed down a road, looking at the 18-wheeler, now in front of it, on the opposite road, while Johnny drives behind it, with Costas and Franco shooting at the remaining two vehicles.

Jorge heaves the last rocket launcher onto his right shoulder, aims, and fires the rocket. The driver of the 18-wheeler panics, but, can't move, knowing that, if he jumps from the truck at his current speed, he'll die anyway. Not to mention the oncoming traffic. He simply watches as the rocket nears.

EXPLOSION!!!

A shower of open and roasting kilos rain down as Johnny turns right to avoid a collision, and the rear bumper of his truck bumps one of his attacker's cars, sending it into another car, which plows directly into its side.

Johnny sees his cohorts and makes a very wide, swift, and dangerous U-turn, speeding until he catches up to them. Everybody looks at each vehicle, confirming all is well with collective head nods.

Scene 22-2:57 P.M. Zion-More plays as a split-screen reveals Vibora, speaking on the phone with an unknown Dock Supervisor.

Supervisor:

Don Jefe, your merchandise should've made it by now, this is routine.

Vibora:

What've you heard?

Supervisor:

Nothing.

As if on cue, Vibora gets another call.

Vibora:

Did my other package arrive?

Supervisor:

Yes, sir.

Vibora:

Hold on.

He presses a button, and a third screen appears, displaying Aaron, looking at a smoldering truckload of his boss's cocaine as it cooks in the middle of the road.

Vibora:

Speak.

Aaron:

Boss, your shipments aren't going to make it.

Vibora:

Why's that?

Aaron:

We're watching one of the trucks go up in flames. And, we just drove by to other truck, also burning.

Vibora's eyes go wide, livid, but his voice remains silky after he exhales heavily.

Aaron:

What do you want us to do, boss?

Vibora:

If you can't magically make my cocaine come back to me from those ashes, there's nothing you can do, just go to the docks and make sure that other package makes it to its destination, not in flames.

Vibora presses a button, ending the call, and flings the phone, causing it to shatter as it hits the wall. Vibora grabs a bottle of Scotch, pours a shot and downs it quickly, pouring another.

Vibora:

Goddamn black American!

3:43 P.M.: Sonrisa and Anita sit next to each other on the couch, Marcos sits in Anita's lap, as Miguel occupies Sonrisa's, Daniel Santacruz-Lento plays softly throughout.

Sonrisa:

Don't tell Steve. No matter what.

Anita:

Why not?! This is his fault!

Sonrisa:

No, mi amor, don't say that.

Anita:

It is, Mama, and you know it! He should've just let Vibora say whatever and ignored him.

Sonrisa:

When you truly love someone, it's impossible to let anyone disrespect or mistreat them. You'll understand one day, nina. Not to mention, Vibora is a bully, and he only started back harassing me after all of these years, because I'm finally happy, for the first time in my life. He left me alone when I was single with three ninos, and as soon as I found Steve, he pops up, like the snake he's named after, only to bring me pain, once again. Please don't say anything to Steve, hija, promise me?

Anita looks at her mother with a hint of defiance, but reluctantly relents.

Anita:

I promise, Mama.

Sonrisa:

Swear to me.

Anita:

I swear.

Sonrisa:

Plus, I have a feeling that, we'll be avenged. Steve was sent to us for a reason. I can feel it.

A knock at the door gently rocks them from their conversation. Miguel slides from Sonrisa's lap as she budges to answer the door. Sonrisa looks at her children.

Sonrisa:

I wonder who this could be. (She reaches the door.) Who is it?

A little girl answers her.

Girl:

Anabella.

Sonrisa opens the door a crack, peeks down,, and spots a pretty, but very dirty little girl of around four or five years of age, and instantly melts as her eyes water. She opens the door fully and kneels down.

Anabella:

Is this the house where the kids with no mama and papa come to live?

Sonrisa cries as she pulls the little girl to her bosom, saying repeatedly…

Sonrisa:

Yes, it is, pequena, yes, it is.

Anita hoists Marcos onto her hip as she and Miguel both rise and join them at the door.

Anabella:

Are those my new brothers and sister?

A fresh burst of tears erupt from Sonrisa as she squeezes Anabella.

Sonrisa:

Yes, hija, we're your new family, now.

Anabella:

I can call you Mama, now?

Sonrisa:

Yes, nina.

Anabella:

Where's Papa?

Sonrisa:

He'll be home in a minute. Come in so that you can get clean and take a bath.

She stands and lets Anabella enter, closing then door behind her. Sonrisa and Anita lock eyes.

Anita:

How'd she find out about us?

Sonrisa:

He's made us famous. The rich black American who married a stripper and ex-prostitute, who found two orphaned children, She probably started asking around, and was miraculously led to us, and safely.

Anita:

Seeing her is making me feel better, already.

Sonrisa:

That's how it feels when you rescue someone who truly needs to be rescued. That's how I felt when I first found you, and when we found Miggy. And, I think this is how Steve felt, and feels, when he met me, met you all, and just dove into this family, head first. He loved me, and started not only rescuing us all, but protecting us. I wonder what he's doing, right now.

Jory ft. Amareto-Dartelo Hoy plays in Freddie's club as a shirtless Steve bleeds from the two holes in his shoulder. Costas comes up behind him, and pours Vodka on the exit wound, then the entrance wound, Steve screams briefly as his eyes bulge.

Steve:

Stupid bastard! Warn a motherfucker, first!

Everybody laughs, with the exception of Steve. Freddie and Raul both heat knives over a burning eye on the stove until the tips are red. Johnny pulls a seat in front of Steve, sits, and beckons…

Johnny:

Steve, look at me, hermano.

Johnny grabs Steve's wrist, holding them down, and stares intensely into his eyes.

Steve:

Johnny, what's wrong, slick?

Johnny:

Forgive me, for what I'm about to say to you, mi amigo.

Steve:

Whatever, asshole!

Johnny smiles at him impishly as Freddie and Raul approach, hot blades raised, as Franco drinks a beer at the bar, watching, silently anticipating.

Johnny:

(to Steve) Mi hermano, really, that wife of your's, how does that pussy of hers taste?

Johnny smiles, then laps his tongue in Steve's face quickly, simulating cunnilingus. Johnny tightens his grip as Steve tries to rise angrily, but is speedily dropped as both knife tips sizzle on his skin, cauterizing the wounds.

Franco winces as Steve takes a deep breath after the knives are removed.

Steve:

You dirty-ass Brazilians!

Costas:

Whoa, papi, don't ever call a Colombian a Brazilian.

Steve:

Why not?!

Johnny:

They know what they did.

Everyone but Steve laughs. Costas says into Steve's left ear…

Costas:

BOO!!!

…and pours a fresh coat of vodka on the freshly closed wounds. Steve gains his composure, staring menacingly at Costas.

Costas:

(feigning surprise and taking a swig from the bottle of vodka) What, I warned you that time, amigo.

Costas hands Steve the vodka, and Steve takes a big chug.

Jonny:

You never answered my question, mi hermano.

Steve:

Don't get shot, muchacho.

Steve hands Johnny the vodka.

Steve:

Take me home, now.

Freddie:

We have one more mission to accomplish.

Steve:

What?!

Franco:

Oh, we won't be blowing these up.

Franco grins, using his hands to simulate, squeezing breasts, as Costas and Johnny both act as if they're grabbing a lady's rear end and flashing their tongues as if they're kissing their imaginary women, Freddie and Raul laugh as Steve puts his bloody shirt back on, then pops the cap from a bottle of beer.

Freddie:

I told you, mi amigo, I'm not a pimp, and, I refuse to turn my club into a brothel.

Steve:

Well, now that that's settled…

He upends the bottle, emptying it with a few big gulps, places it on the bar, and says…

Steve:

Let's get physical!

Ivy Queen-La Vida Es Asi plays throughout the montage as Sonrisa and Anita give Anabella a bath, wash her hair, and playfully splash water at her and each other, laughing as they do. Sonrisa hurriedly wipes an errant tear as it rolls down her cheek. Anita grabs her right hand and squeezes it upon noticing this, and Sonrisa smiles at her. Anabella notices this and scoots toward Sonrisa, comforting her.

Anabella:

Don't cry, Mama.

Sonrisa:

(rubbing both of her daughter's cheeks) I'm just so happy, mis ninas. (looking at Anabella You're so sweet, Anabella.

Anabella:

Gracias.

Sonrisa:

(to Anita) Isn't your hermanita so sweet, 'Nita?

Anita:

(rubbing Anabella's hair) Yes, she is. And. I finally have a little sister.

Sonrisa:

(tickling Anabella) And, the boys don't outnumber us anymore.

They all laugh at this.

Show Sonrisa and Anita dressing Anabella in a shirt of Anita's that covers her completely, being too large for her.

Show them both brushing and fiddling with her hair.

Meanwhile: Tito El Bambino-Caile plays throughout the scene as Jesus drives behind an all-white truck. The truck has two occupants, 1 driver and passenger. Jesus, as well as the driver of the truck, are completely oblivious to Ferdinand and Jorge on their right; Freddie, Raul, with Steve nursing an AK-47 while lying on his back in the cab, coming up on their rear, and Johnny, Franco, and Costas in the cab, laying on his back, holding an AR-15, coming up on their left.

Jorge gets out of the passenger seat, wielding a .9mm Desert Eagle in his right hand, and looks at Freddie, who slaps his door, alerting Steve, who sits up like a vampire with his AK-47 at the ready. He immediately spots a family of six, one father, mother, two boys, and two girls, all staring at him, he only nods and pans the area left to right, seeing a police car. This prompts him to stand and stare down the two officers. The passenger reaches for the radio, fearfully bringing the speaker to his mouth; Steve follows suit by holding up his chrome AK-47, staring down the officer, who holds his right hand up in surrender, while using his left hand to place the radio back on its receiver.

Costas pops up, just as Franco and Raul exit the passenger seats. Jorge races toward the white truck, gun raised, Jesus panics, jabs the horn repeatedly. Stop, as the barrel of an M-16 is placed on his left cheek by Raul, who tells Aaron in the passenger seat...

Raul:

Put both of your fucking hands up!

Aaron does as he is told.

Raul:

How many in back?

Jesus:

Three.

Raul:

(yelling to the back) Don't you move, or mi amigo will kill you all, hold your hands up! (to Jesus and Aaron) You two, get the fuck in the back! (to Franco) It's clear, hermano.

Franco slides the van door pointing a Mac-11 at all five men, who have their hands raised in fear.

Jorge opens the passenger door to the white truck, immediately blowing the passenger's brains onto the driver, then blowing the driver's brains out of his window, sending chunks of his brain and blood onto the hood of the next car. Jorge heaves the passenger's body out of the car and onto the road, pulls the door closed, and opens the driver side door, kicking the driver's corpse into the street.

The two officers look bewildered, but dare not move against men who will clearly murder them, as Steve simply stares at them, holding his AK-47, clothed in his bloody shirt.

Jorge proceeds to drive, with all three of his accomplices in tow.

Meanwhile: Show Sonrisa, Anita, and Anabella cooking, while Miguel sets the table, and Marcos runs around with his ball.

6:17 P.M.: Jorge slowly leads his entourage into a jungle, coming to a complete stop.

Raul and Franco escort Jesus and his four partners out of the vehicle as Jorge, Steve, Johnny, Costas, Freddie, and Ferdinand all make their way to the truck. Jorge pulls the latch left to right, and turns the handle, tossing the door up, revealing sixteen teenage girls, all dressed in slightly tattered clothing and all cowering away from the armed men, who now stare at them incredulously. Steve and Freddie both jump into the cab, raising their hands, saying to the ladies…

Steve:

Calm down, chicas, calm down. We're here to help you. Whatever you thought you were going to have to do, you don't have to do now. Whatever men have been doing to you, none of us will do. I'm married, and these gentlemen aren't animals or rapists.

Freddie:

I think you all were supposed to come and be forced to work in my club.

The thing is, I'm not a pimp, and, I only want women working in my establishment who want and choose to be there. So, we're going to find you all somewhere to sleep, eat, and get cleaned up. If you're from Colombia, you're in Cali; if not, we'll try our best to get you back wherever you're from.

Steve looks at the five men that Raul and Franco hold at gunpoint, and makes a beeline toward them, with a severe look in his eyes. Upon arrival, Raul looks at him, asking…

Raul:

What's wrong, mi amigo?

Steve looks angrily at all five men, but puts his face an inch away Jesus'.

Steve:

I don't know what it is about you creepy ass dudes, but, for some odd reason I have an uncontrollable urge to kill you all. (to Raul and Franco) Mis hermanos, take a few steps back.

Franco steps to Steve, placing his hand on his shoulder.

Franco:

Steve, you have to calm down, amigo. Your nose is bleeding.

Steve wipes his nose with his already bloody shirt.

Steve:

I told you, Frankie, for some strange reason, I have to kill them. I've never felt a stronger urge to do something in my entire life. It feels as if, I don't kill them right this minute, if I try to leave this spot without doing that, I'll drop dead.

210

The look of intensity in Steve's eyes backs Franco away from him.   Steve pulls the switch on the AK-47, enabling it to only shoot single bursts, and goes down the line, putting the barrel between each man's eyes, blowing their brains out. Upon killing the last man, Blake, a feeling of extreme completion and ecstasy overcomes Steve, as a split-screen reveals Sonrisa in their kitchen, raising her head as she catches a deep shiver, and fiddles with her crucifix, as Steve drops to his knees, breathing heavily.

Scene 23-7:23 P.M.: Sonrisa and the children sit around the table, eating and laughing, with Marcos sitting in his highchair between Sonrisa and Anita, when Steve walks in and sits down, smiling at his family, as they all look at his blood-stained shirt, wide-eyed and slack-jawed. Upon Steve sitting, Sonrisa rises, but, Steve signals her to stay seated, so as not to alarm the children.

Anabella:

Papa, you're bleeding.

Steve:

I was bleeding, princess. I'm okay, now. And your name is?

Anabella:

Anabella.

Steve:

(tickling her neck, making her laugh) That's funny.

Anabella:

What?

Steve:

You say Anabella, but all I heard was princess.

Anabella beams as Steve smiles at her. Sonrisa looks at Steve with a look of wonder, as she reaches under the table, grabbing Anita's hand, and they share a squeeze. Anita can't help but smile at Steve.

Sonrisa:

Mi amor, are you hungry?

Steve:

Very much so, angelita. (to Anabella) Has your big brother been mean to you?

Anabella:

No.

Steve looks at Miguel suspiciously, while still speaking to Anabella.

Steve:

You sure he hasn't threatened you in order to keep you silent?

Anabella:

Yes.

Steve:

He looks rather shifty, to me. I think I'm going to spank him, anyway.

Anabella:

(laughing as Steve reaches for Miguel) No, papito, don't spank him.

Steve:

It's too late for that, princess. (reaching playfully for a laughing and squirming Miguel) Come here, Miggy!

Miguel:

(laughing) No, Papa. I didn't do anything.

Sonrisa:

Leave my son alone.

Steve:

He knows what he did. (to Anabella) What about Miss Colombiana, your big sister, she's been nice to you?

Anabella:

Yes, she did my hair.

Sonrisa:

I helped, nina.

Anabella:

And Mama helped.

Steve:

No wonder it looks so pretty.

Anita:

What happened to your arm, Steve?

Steve:

Nothing major.

Sonrisa sits a plate in front of Steve, which he immediately starts to devour, as Sonrisa places a bottled beer in front of him, asking...

Sonrisa:

(gently touching his shoulder after noticing the blood on the back of his shirt) Mi Diablito, are you sure you're okay?

Steve:

Look at me, don't I look fine? Don't worry, Sunny. Freddie and I fixed it. When I take a shower—

Sonrisa:

—We take a shower.

Steve:

(grinning) We'll clean it, bandage it. Presto!

They kiss, to Anabella's amusement.

Meanwhile: 7:57 P.M.: Elvis Crespo-Yo No Soy Un Monstruo plays as Vibora paces back and forth in his office, while holding a ringing phone. A split-screen reveals the dead bodies of Jesus and his bandits, being eaten by wolves in the jungle, as Jesus's phone just rings in his pocket.

Vibora presses about three buttons, a faint ringing is heard, when an unknown male voice answers.

Male:

Si, patron?

Vibora:

Send the next crew.

Meanwhile: 8:03 P.M.: Steve finishes his food and says to Anabella…

Steve:

Did Mama tell you that she has a nino in her belly?

Anabella:

Mama's pregnant?!

Steve:

Yes, I hope it's a boy.

Anabella:

A girl.

Steve:

(tickling her) A boy.

Anabella:

(laughing) girl.

They go back and forth a few times.

Steve:

(holding up his hands in mock surrender) Okay, okay, you win, you win. Let's just agree that we all want a boy, and stop arguing.

Everybody laughs or smile. Anita's phone rings, and, one can tell by the shy look as she ducks her head and talk, that it's Paulo.

Miguel:

(making kissing noises at Anita) I love you, mi novio, Paulo, mi amor.

Steve:

I suddenly have a strong urge to take out my knife and remove Paulo's—

Sonrisa shoots him a look and glances at Anabella, as Anita covers the mouthpiece of the phone.

Anabella:

Remove Paulo's what, papito?

Steve:

You'll find out the minute you start having boyfriends. (He winks and grins at Anabella, who laughs as Sonrisa smiles at them.)

Sonrisa:

Diablo!

Steve:

Diablo needs a shower.

Sonrisa:

El Diablo always needs a cleansing.

Steve:

And an angel makes everything clean. Care to join me?

Sonrisa:

(smiling impishly) I thought you'd never ask.

Miguel and Anabella smile and giggle at each other knowingly, as Anita rolls her eyes and leaves the table. Sonrisa lifts Marcos from his highchair and sits him on the floor. He follows Anita.

In the bathroom, Steve winces as he tries to remove his shirt, Sonrisa rushes to his aid.

Sonrisa:

You must tell me, mi marido, Mi Diablito, what happened to you, and what did you do?

Steve:

I didn't do much. I just liberated sixteen teenage girls who would've been Vibora's future prostitutes, you, if no one else in the world, understands what it feels like to be one of his, shall we say, playthings against your will, so, you should understand why I'd set those ladies free, having rescued you, in a manner of speaking. I also sabotaged two truckloads of Vibora's cocaine, which, would've ruined many lives. I know, I know, all he'll do is grow more, and sell more; a delay can change many things, hopefully for the better. And, I'm the only one who got shot in the process.

Sonrisa:

(crying and touching his wound) Mi heroe, you could've died, you have to be more careful. (She kisses him.)

Steve:

We are well beyond 'careful' and 'retreat' now, mi amor. We're in it, now. There's only two ways out of this.

Sonrisa:

Win or die.

Steve:

The funny thing about that is, we may have to do one, in order to do the other. Will you be ready if that day comes?

Sonrisa:

Will you be by my side?

Steve:

Always.

Sonrisa:

Then I'll always be ready. (She takes his pants and underwear down, taking a step back, allowing her nightgown to fall to the floor. She steps to him sliding her tongue into his mouth, and uses her hand expertly on his cock.) Now let's see about making the pain go away.

On their front step, Anita and Paulo kiss. Paulo slowly moves his hand up her nightgown, discovering she wears no underwear.

Anita:

Mi amor, I need you to take away my bad memories.

Paulo:

What happened took place only hours ago…

Anita:

Don't speak of it. Just tell me if you really meant what you said about falling in love with me.

Paulo:

With all of my heart.

Anita:

Take me.

Anita reaches into his pants, pulling out his erection, and spreads her legs. Behind the door, Miguel, Anabella, and Marcos have their ears pressed against the door, eavesdropping.

Anabella:

What're they doing, Miggy?

Miguel:

They're doing what Mama and Papa do.

Anabella:

(Her eyes widen from shock.) Making sex!

Miguel:

Shh, hermanita. Yes, sex.

In the bathroom, Sonrisa has Steve pinned against a wall as the shower runs on her back.

Sonrisa:

Mi guerrero, out there, starting a war, risking his life for me, getting shot for me.

She licks down his chest until his fully erect penis is in her mouth causing him to close his eyes and tilt his head back.

Steve:

If you stay down there much longer, you'll be the one getting shot.

Sonrisa:

(in English) That's what I'm hoping for. ( resuming fellatio) Callate, papi, let me do this.

Frankie J ft. Baby Bash-Obsession (No Es Amor) plays throughout the scene. On the front step, Anita moans into Paulo's ear as he softly grunts into her, squeezing her buttocks as his pants fall to his ankles.

A split-screen reveals Steve holding Sonrisa against the wall, in the same position, delivering repeated thrusts into his wife, as Paulo does the same to his daughter. After a few more strokes, Paulo ejaculates into Anita, audibly, with three sharp drives into her, kissing Anita as he finishes.

Paulo:

I love you, Anita.

Anita:

I love you, mi amor.

Steve and Sonrisa's screen slides into full view, and Steve rams into Sonrisa as he comes, sticking his tongue into her mouth, which she hungrily accepts. Anita kisses Paulo one last time, telling him…

Anita:

I have to go, call me tomorrow.

Paulo:

Okay.

Inside, Miguel grabs Anabella and Marcos by their arms and speeds off down the hallway.

Scene 24-9:51 P.M.: Vibora sits in his office, surrounded by ten new men, speaking with the two policemen who witnessed (or were escorting) his truck of women get hijacked by Steve, as Baby Rasta Y Gringo-Me Niegas plays.

Vibora:

You sure it was them?

Officer #1:

He's the only black American in this part of Cali. And, who here doesn't know Freddie, his brothers, and their two cousins?

Vibora:

(slapping his right palm on the desk) And, yet, you did nothing?!

Officer #2:

It was only two of us, and we were heavily outgunned.

Vibora:

I can understand that. (He walks to his window and peers out.) I don't know what it is about this American that, not only did he choose a whore with three bastards to marry, he also got Freddie, of all people, to defy me. (He walks back to his desk.) Now, I hate involving kids in this shit...unless they're my whores and strippers.

A chorus of light chuckles affirms agreement.

Vibora:

Or the ninos that run my drugs. But, other than that....

(He downs a shot that sat on his desk and states menacingly at the camera.)

Meanwhile: An overhead shot of Miguel and Marcos' room shows them sleeping soundly and fades into a shot of Anita and Anabella, sharing Anita's bed, both asleep, with Anita's arm draped over Anabella.

Steve and Sonrisa talk as Steve lies on his right side, holding Sonrisa, who rubs the flesh around Steve's entrance wound. Los Playas-Tan Cerca Y Tan Lejos plays softly throughout the scene.

Sonrisa:

You do know that I fell deeper in love with you tonight, don't you, Mi Diablito?

Steve:

After what I did to you in the shower, I'm not surprised. (He smiles at her as she swats his arm.)

Sonrisa:

That's not what I'm talking about, Diablo!

Steve:

Then what?

Sonrisa:

You do know that we have another child, don't you?

Steve:

How could I not? I talked to her.

Sonrisa:

How come you acted as if you didn't notice?

Steve:

How was I supposed to act? Would you rather I acted as if I was so shocked and appalled by her presence, that she wouldn't've felt as if we didn't want her here, or made her so uncomfortable that she would've felt uneasy and guilty about being here? Or, would you prefer that I do what I did and make her feel welcomed, like you would've done had the roles been reversed?

Sonrisa:

(rubbing his face, pecking his lips) I love you, mi marido.

Steve:

I love you, too, mi esposa.

Sonrisa:

Why didn't you ask her where she came from, or how she found us, or how she got here?!

Steve:

For the same reason you didn't ask her all of those things.

Sonrisa:

How do you know I didn't ask her all of those things?

Steve:

Because I know mi mujer. You just want babies and babies and more babies and to help them all. I'll bet the first thing you did when you saw her, was cry, didn't you?

Sonrisa:

(wiping tears from her face) She looked so sweet when I opened the door. So dirty, so scared, so nervous, and so hopeful. I just broke down.

Steve:

(pulling her to him) She just showed up at the doorstep. Now you see why I didn't ask her what she went through or how she got here. Whatever she went through, it was horrible enough for her to hear a whisper of a rumor about a lady who took in two orphans, have a baby of her own, only to marry an American, who embraced them all. She was so low, that she would roam Cali, all alone, asking where you were, even if you didn't exist, on faith that you did, hoping that, if you did, you'd take pity on her. And, what happened? She ended up on our doorstep. So, in short, the way I see it, after going through what she's been through, she must belong here. She's here. Who am I to question why or how? I felt good making her laugh and feel good. She acts as if she's been here forever. She has to belong here, she just has to.

Sonrisa:

( crying harder now) My good little Devil.

Thunder booms and lightning flashes outside as a downpour of rain follows. A few seconds later, several knocks on the door cause Sonrisa to dry her eyes.

Anabella:

Mama, Papa, we're scared.

Sonrisa:

Come in, mis ninos.

All four children storm the bed. Sonrisa lets Anita and Marcos lay in front of her, while Anabella lies by Steve, with Miguel in the middle.

Sonrisa:

( touching Anabella's nose, making her smile) Daddy's girl.

They smile at one another. Steve and Sonrisa pull the blanket over themselves and their children, and complete the covering by interlocking their fingers, embracing all four children, smiling at each other.

A time lapse occurs, revealing the sun rising. Steve and Sonrisa still hold hands, but Anita is on her back, with Marcos' upper body sprawled onto her, and Miguel lies on his stomach, while Anabella now faces Steve.

Act 7-Scene 24: Alexis Y Fido-Donde Estes Llegares plays throughout as Vibora walks down a dark flight of stairs. The flip of a switch shines light on an all-white basement, which is clearly a torture chamber, equipped with two hospital beds, with leg and arm restraints, handcuffs and straps dangle from hooks on the ceiling, four clearly starving pit bulls bark at their master as they pace, through their corner cage, ribcages visible. Various tools for cutting or poking hang like macabre pool cues, lining the wall immediately to his left.

Vibora:

(speaking to his dogs) FOOD is on the way, mis animales. Food is on the way.

Meanwhile: Vibora's ten bandits kick the door in to Freddie's apartment, revealing a living room with four sleeping men; Franco, Costas, Ferdinand, and Raul. Franco reaches for his waist, but a man with a sawed-off double barrel shotgun is on top of him, blowing the top half of his head and face off, as both barrels blast. Four men rush to the other rooms, various weapons raised. The man in the middle kicks the bathroom door open, exposing a shitting Johnny. The two men who turn right, open a door, revealing Freddie, laying on his back, while an anonymous woman rides him. The man on the right shoots her in the head.

Freddie:

What the fuck?! That was my wife!

Gunman:

You'll be with her soon enough. Put your fucking clothes on!

The man who turns left opens a door, showing Jorge aiming a .45 at the door, firing three times, hitting the man in the face with all three shots, as he readies himself, seeing multiple shadows. A voice calls to him.

Male:

It's three of us, and, when we turn this corner, we're all shooting assault rifles, the next move is yours.

Jorge:

You're the one talking, so, I guess I'll be taking you with me.

The three men turn the corner, and, proving himself a psychic, shoots the talking gunman one time in his throat, before being stitched in the face and torso with a barrage of bullets, which mangle him beyond recognition as he falls backward. The gunman with the neck wound stares up at his partner, who pulls a .357 Magnum from his waist, aims at his wounded partner's head, and fires once between his eyes. The screen goes black.

Scene 25-Steve walks home, with Miguel and Anabella, holding four grocery bags, while his son and daughter eat candy. Sonrisa's eight "friends" all exit Bethany's house, adjusting their breasts, touching their hair, and smoothing their clothes, approaching their prey with celerity. Steve smiles at them all.

Steve:

Ladies, ladies, how're you all doing? You all look nice, today.

All eight ladies giggle and thank him simultaneously.

Sara:

(to Miguel) Hola, Miggy, are you going to introduce us to your new friend?

Anabella:

(angrily) I'm his little sister, now, stop rubbing on my father!

Carmen, Rosalita, and Ilanny stop groping Steve, but not the flirtatious banter.

Ilanny:

We were just saying how we wish a man would start a war with a drug lord over us.

Steve:

Keep hope alive.

Everyone but the kids laugh, oblivious to a scowling Sonrisa, who watches this from her living room window, as Anita talks on the phone to Paulo. Sonrisa walks quickly to the kitchen, opens a drawer, extracts a butcher knife, and speeds out of the door, causing Anita to get excited and watch her mother out of the window, giving Paulo a play-by-play.

Wisin Y Yandel-Abusadora begins as Sonrisa walks angrily toward her husband, children, and the brood of witches, posing as women, who masquerade as her friends. Steve notices the knife too late, as Sonrisa slices Bethany's cheek, from eye to chin.

Sonrisa:

Perra, you keep touching and rubbing mi marido, I'm going to kill you!!!

Anabella:

I told these malditas to leave mi papa alone, mamita.

Miguel just laughs.

Sonrisa:

(talking to Anabella, slowly approaching Steve, with the knife raised inches from his nose) I know you did, mi nina. But, your father isn't completely innocent. (to Steve) Take our children home, Steve!

Steve looks his wife squarely in the eyes, and obeys, leaving her to argue briefly with her sliced-up friend, and the rest of the ladies. His phone vibrates and he retrieves it from his pocket, presses a button, and reads a text from Freddie, as complete shock and horror cover his face, his eyes and mouth opening wide.

Miguel:

What's wrong, Papa?

Steve:

Nothing, hijo.

Upon entering the house, Anita ends her conversation with Paulo.

Anita:

I'll see you later, mi amor. (She presses the END button on her phone, placing it into her pocket as she approaches Steve.) Did Mama cut Bethany?!

Miguel:

You should've seen it, hermana!

Steve:

Calmate, Miggy. (to Anita) Come with me, 'Nita.

All three children look apprehensively at Steve.

Anita:

What's wrong, Steve?

Steve:

Nothing, I—

Sonrisa barges into the house and heads straight for Steve.

Sonrisa:

(waving the knife in his face) How dare you flirt with those dirty bitches, filthy swine!!!

Steve:

First of all—

Sonrisa:

CAILATE!!! ( She slaps him.

Steve rubs his jaw, exhaling heavily, and looks at the children as Marcos stumbles in, rubbing his eyes. He looks at Anita, who picks him up.

Anabella

Mama, Papa, please don't fight?!

Steve:

(to Sonrisa) You need to calm down!

She pokes his gunshot wound, which causes him to wince angrily and grabs her by the arm. The kids collectively protest. Anabella runs between them, holding her arms up to Steve.

Anabella:

Papa, pick me up, don't fight!

Steve picks her up, never taking his eyes off of his knife-wielding esposa.

Steve:

(to Anabella) Princess, besame. (Princesa, kiss me.)

Anabella pecks his lips. Steve looks at Anita.

Steve:

'Nita, take them to the movies or something. Can you get Paulo to go with you?

Anita:

Yes. Please don't argue.

Anabella:

Don't fight, Papa.

Steve:

Princess, trust me, this isn't going to be much of a fight. (He winks slyly at Sonrisa.)

Anabella notices this, and reaches for Sonrisa.

Sonrisa:

DIABLO!!!

Anabella:

Give me to Mama!

Sonrisa:

Give me our nina!

Steve laughs at the conspiracy.

Steve:

(to Sonrisa) She's smart. She gets that from my side of the family.

Steve starts the children toward the door, with Anabella squeezing him, starting to cry.

Anabella:

No, Papa, no. I don't want to go.

Steve:

(reaching around his neck, removing the crucifix Sonrisa gave him) Calm down, pequena (baby girl), see this?

Anabella:

Si, it's pretty, Papa.

Steve:

Mama gave this to me, and, I want you to wear it today. It's my promise to you that, when you get back home, me and Mama will be happy, again.

Anabella:

You promise?

Steve:

I swear.

They peck lips. He approaches Sonrisa, removes her crucifix, which she touches, but lets him remove. He puts it on Anita, who looks at Sonrisa, who smiles at her.

Anita:

What's wrong, Steve?!

Steve:

Nothing. (He reaches into his pocket, pulling a wad of money from it, peeling off a few bills and handing them to Anita.) Go have fun.

Steve dries Anita's and Anabella's tears and ushers the kids from the house. Steve turns, facing his wife stoically, poker-faced, with his arms folded.

A split-screen shows Sonrisa's angry glare, and Steve's blank stare, as a powder blue graffiti caption under Sonrisa's face reads, 'Angelita' vs., a red graffiti caption under Steve's face reads 'Diablito.' A golden halo appears over Sonrisa's head, as red horns appear on the sides of Steve's head. The split-screen and captions vanish upward in a puff of smoke as Steve makes his way to Sonrisa with three giant steps, pushing her forehead violently with his forefinger.

Steve:

I think you're going to need another knife, Pretty One.

He smiles at her, knowing.

Sonrisa:

I HATE THAT NAME!!! DIABLO, DON'T CALL ME THAT!!!

Steve:

I don't give a fuck what you hate! I hate when my wife waits until I'm wounded, to attack me, slap me, and wave a fucking knife in my face in front of our kids, Pretty One.

He bumps her shoulder hard as he storms past her, smiling, until he feels the knife slice down his right shoulder blade. He looks up with the blank stare and slight grin of a lunatic, as the horns appear and vanish quickly. He opens a drawer and removes another butcher knife, identical to the one she now holds

Steve:

You'd better take this, because, when I'm through with you, you're going to wish you'd've stabbed me, instead of sliced me, Pretty One. (tossing the knife at her feet) Besides, Vibora knew beauty when he saw it. I mean, clearly, you are pretty.

Sonrisa:

CALLATE, DIABLO, CALLATE!!! (She tears up and picks up the knife.)

Outside, all four Jerez-Davis children have their ears to the door, eyes wide in anticipation. Anabella asks no one in particular...

Anabella:

Do they fight a lot?!

Miguel:

This is their first fight, hermanita.

Inside, Steve resumes his taunting.

Steve:

It's funny, but, even when you call me 'Little Devil' now, especially now, you holding those knives, looking mean as hell, sexy, I get an erection. But it's ironic, that, the Devil is exactly what I'm about to show you.

Steve reaches and turns a small radio on that sits next to the sink, Juanes-La Luz plays from the beginning.

Steve:

We need music, for this dance.

Sonrisa:

Don't do this, mi marido, I'm pregnant, our child.

Steve:

That's exactly why I'm not going to hit you below the neck. All head-shots, like close-up pictures. And, you should've thought about that before you slapped and sliced me.

Steve runs toward her, but stops short when she fends him off with an aerial slice from each hand. He dips back after she narrowly misses him, and throws a right across her face, slapping the tip of her nose. She looks at him, shocked, but now recognizes that he is dead set on a fight. She looks at him, eyes narrowing, as she holds both knives up, blades inward.

Steve:

There's mi angelita.

Steve holds his hands at his waist, bobbing and weaving slowly, baiting his wife to take a swipe. His movements become rhythmic to the music. Sonrisa charges, but is caught on her left jaw by his open right hand, causing blood to fly from her inner jaw. She swings wildly with her right hand, slicing his inner right forearm as it descends. He comes clean across her right jaw with his left hand, making her drop the knife in her right hand. Then, he raises his right hand (It's slo-mo, as he grimaces, coming down with all of his might across her face, normal speed just before he makes contact, a loud smack is heard as he comes down on her left eye, making her drop the knife as she falls to the ground. He stands over her.)

Steve:

You know what happens now, don't you?

Sonrisa:

( crying, pleading) You win, mi marido, I'm sorry!!!

Steve:

( dropping to his knees, pulling her legs, dragging her to him) Don't be sorry, now!

He reaches up her skirt, snatching her panties off.

Sonrisa:

No, Mi Diablito, don't do this to me!!! Not you, not this!!!

Steve:

Shut up, bitch!!! Should've thought of that before you cut me. I could've overlooked the slap, but not the blade.

She makes a quick attempt at his eyes, but he secures both of her hands, pinning them over her head. He reaches down and undoes his pants, freeing himself.

Steve:

You ready for this, Angelita?!

Sonrisa:

(screaming out) SOMEBODY HELP ME!!! PLEASE, MI MARIDO, NOT YOU, ANYBODY BUT MI ESPOSO!!!

Steve looks down on her, and his eyes go from fury to sympathy as her face becomes the fifteen-year-old version of herself. He closes his eyes, and, in a vain effort to shake it off, still sees the image.

Outside the door, Anita holds Marcos as Anabella tells Miguel…

Anabella:

Papa's going to kill Mama!!! We have to help her!

Anita:

SHHH, hermanita, listen. They're quiet now. They might make up.

Inside, Sonrisa calms down and rubs Steve's face, trying to stop him from violating her as Juanes'-La Luz, fades into Shakira's Addicted to You, which plays throughout.

Sonrisa:

You win, mi amor, you win. I surrender. (She pecks him with kisses all over his face.) You win, Diablo, tocame, tocame! ( She kisses his lips and smiles when he responds by kissing her in return.) Mi amor, I knew you wouldn't violate me. Tocame, papi, tocame!

They kiss, this time, exchanging tongues, as Sonrisa takes his right hand and guides it between her legs. She moans heavily and bites his ear, saying into it...

Sonrisa:

Aye, Dios Mio, papi, I love you, so much, mi amor. Thank you for not violating me. I'm so sorry for hurting you, mi marido. I'm sorry, come to me.

She puts her arms around his neck and lays on her back, pulling him down with her.

Sonrisa:

Hablame, mi marido. (Talk to me, my husband.) Tell me you love me, Mi Diablito.

He looks down on her as she puts her hand on his chest, and her face materializes into her present self.

Steve:

I love you, mi angelita.

Sonrisa:

Take me, Diablito.

He enters her, and she tilts her head back, exhaling heavily, and gripping his buttocks.

Outside the door, Anita eases her younger siblings.

Anita:

I told you they were going to make up. Listen.

Paulo comes up from behind them, scaring them audibly.

Paulo:

What're they doing?

Anabella:

Making sex.

Everybody laughs. Paulo and Anita kiss.

Anita:

Let's take them to a movie, mi amor.

Paulo:

Let's go.

Inside, Sonrisa is now bent over, breasts swinging freely, as Steve strokes her from behind. She leans back and they share a ravenous kiss as Steve fondles her breasts, then slides his right hand to her clit, causing her to bite her bottom lip.

Meanwhile: The kids are completely unaware of the black van that follows them.

Meanwhile: Sonrisa is on top of Steve, bouncing away, as Steve palms her ass with both hands. A split-screen shows the black van coming up behind the five kids just as Steve ejaculates into Sonrisa. She leans down and they kiss as she continues to move her hips, and four men jump out of the van, two snatch Miguel and Marcos, while Paulo pushes Anita and Anabella, tripping one of the men, and shoving the other, Paulo yells at the ladies to run, pushing them until they run hard, making their way into the woods. The men let them run and get back into the van, which backs up, swerving into a U-turn, and speeds away.

A full-screen reveals a crying Anita and Anabella, being carried by Paulo.

Anita:

(falling to her knees) They took mi hermanitos!!!

Paulo kneels down, and Anabella goes to Anita, who grabs her and kisses her.

Meanwhile: J-Alvarez ft. Arcangel-Regalame Una Noche plays softly throughout the scene as Sonrisa and Steve lay on their sides, facing each other in a lover's embrace. Steve holds her rear with his left hand, as her right leg is over his left.

Sonrisa:

I love you, so much, mi amor. I'm so happy, right now.

Steve:

I love you, too. You have to stop being so jealous, mi amor.

Sonrisa:

I'm sorry, Mi Diablito. But, I'm jealous for a reason.

Steve:

Why? I'm yours, angelita.

Sonrisa:

You just answered your own question. You're mine! You don't understand just how long I've waited for you, prayed and cried for you. Everything I was forced to endure, because, to you, we just fell in love at first sight. But, I hoped a prayed for you, every day since our fifteenth birthday. And, now that I have you, I will kill to keep you. I wish I would let you stray, or let a bitch even think that she can attempt to take you from me, papi. We aren't your average couple. We weren't just made for each other, we were born for each other.

They share a kiss.

Sonrisa:

Don't you get jealous about me, Diablito!

Steve:

Hell yeah! But, we can't just go around slicing and stabbing and shooting and fighting everybody who compliments or flirts with one of us. I take it as a compliment that men may flirt with you. I also know when it's going too far, and, I'll break it up, respectfully. Today, the ladies crossed a line, touching me. But, they only want a good man like you have. She didn't deserve that. You left her scarred for life.

Sonrisa:

Now she knows not to touch my man.

Steve:

So mean, mamacita. (He rubs her clitoris, making her purr.) How can we make the lioness a kitten?

Sonrisa:

Ahem. Just keep on touching me there, papi.

They tongue kiss.

Sonrisa:

Why did you give our necklaces to our ninos?

Steve:

Because, tonight might be our last night together, and, ladies tend to be a little more sentimental. Plus, your crucifix was your mother's. Now, it's your hija's.

Sonrisa;

How do you know this?! Why didn't you tell me? Why did you send our kids away?!

Steve:

I didn't want to worry you, or them. Freddie sent me a text that his brother and cousin got shot to death this morning, and Vibora's men snatched him and the other four. So, knowing that they were coming for us, the safest thing I could do for the kids was give them a head start.

She cries and pulls herself into Steve.

Sonrisa:

My babies.

Steve:

They'll be fine. They have 'Nita. I can only say I'm sorry for putting them in this position. I truly regret that. I should've thought more about them. But, the funny thing is, whenever the man said something derogatory about you, my mind shut down and reprogrammed like the Terminator, and, I just became an animal, hell bent on defending your honor. And, for that, I'll never apologize. I'll do the same thing repeatedly, for eternity if I had to. I love you, mi angelita.

Sonrisa:

(crying harder) I love you, too, Mi Diablito.

They kiss as the front door is kicked open. They continue to kiss, ignoring the men with assault rifles pointed at them. The last man who enters says...

Male:

It looks as if you two won't be resisting.

Steve:

Correcto.

Male:

Shall we?

Steve:

We shall.

Steve pulls his pants up, as Sonrisa hoists her shoulder straps onto her shoulders, covering her exposed breasts. She and Steve rise together, join hands and lead the way out of the house, into the night.

Scene 26-10:37 P.M.: From left to right; Raul, Costas, Ferdinand, Freddie, and Johnny all hang by their handcuffed wrists. The cuffs are held up by ropes that wrap around a pole that will rise when cranked. The men all have broken noses, one or both eyes swollen and/or bleeding, and their swollen lips leak a mixture of saliva and blood.

Miguel's and Marcos' hands are cuffed and tied to a longer rope, as they sit on the floor, unharmed.

The door leading to this torture Chamber opens, and the seven cuffed prisoners look up, seeing feet descend the staircase; then, Steve comes into view, followed closely by Sonrisa, who brightens upon seeing her sons, but becomes furious upon realizing they are restrained. She turns violently on Vibora and his men, rushing Vibora.

Sonrisa:

YOU FUCKING ANIMAL!!! COWARD!!! THEY'RE JUST LITTLE BOYS!!!

Steve grabs Sonrisa around her waist, guiding her to Miguel and Marcos. She runs and kisses them both, crying while checking their wrists for bruises, and their bodies for blood, bruises, or scars, looking briefly in disgust at the hanging men. Steve looks at Vibora condescendingly.

Steve:

Really?! Handcuffing kids?! I see you have a fetish for torturing children, Don Jefe.

Vibora:

I only restrained the boys. I haven't hurt them…yet.

Steve:

(walking to his wife and sons, looking at his hanging comrades) Goddammit, mi hermanos, forgive me. I'm sorry. (He kneels and checks the boys.) I'm sorry, mis ninos. Are you all right?

Miguel:

Si, Papa.

Steve:

We're going to do whatever we have to, to get you two out of here. (whispering) Where are Anita and Anabella?

Miguel:

(whispering) With Paulo, they ran.

Sonrisa exhales and cries, falling into Steve's embrace. Steve rubs Marcos' face.

Vibora:

These beds are for you and your lady. The sooner we get this over with, the better.

Sonrisa kisses her son's multiple times before rising.

Sonrisa:

I love you, so much, mi amores. I love you, so much.

Miguel:

We love you, Mama.

Marcos reaches out for her, and she breaks down all over again. A tear leaves Steve's eye as he holds a bawling Sonrisa. He reaches out and dries Marcos' eyes for nothing, as new tears replace the old ones. Sonrisa screams at Vibora in a complete rage.

Sonrisa:

AAAAAAAAIEHHHHH!!! YOU COWARD SON-OF-A-BITCH!!! THEY'RE JUST LITTLE BOYS!!!

She rushes him, spits in his face, and slaps him three times, drawing blood from his mouth.

Three of his men grab her, while the remaining five aim weapons at Steve. The 3 men escort a struggling Sonrisa to one of the hospital beds, strapping her down.

Vibora:

( looking at Steve, gesturing with his right hand to the remaining bed) Care to take your place next to your wife, like a good husband?

Steve walks to the bed as Vibora snaps his fingers, and two of his goons holster their weapons, and rush to strap Steve on the bed.

Vibora:

I don't think I've ever told either of you the story of how I got my name 'Vibora.' (He visualizes.) When I was a nino my father used to always say, 'My son, don't go into the jungle, nino. There're things that can and will kill you lurking in those trees.' It worked on me for a while, until me, Carlos, and

Chico, my friends that you murdered, were playing in my backyard, and our ball went into the woods. Long story short, we ran into the woods to retrieve the ball, we find it, and, right after that, a viper bites me, right on the left leg. My mother and father sat on my bed, worrying, thinking I would die any minute. Four or five days later, the swelling goes down, my fever breaks, and I went right back to playing, After that, my friends called me 'Vibora.'

Now, about my cocaine. This is Colombia, papi, the air is made of puro. But, that was a lot of fucking money that you and these idiots blew up. Somebody, I think we know who, is going to have to pay for that. And, now, I want my whores. Tell me where you took my whores, and, I'll let your sons go and just kill you and your whore wife. If you don't tell me what you did with my ladies, I'll kill you all, even the boys.

So, what'll it be?

Vibora walks to the wall of many blades and pulls a small pair of gardening shears from a rack. He reaches and presses a button on the wall panel, which causes the bar that holds the seven cuffed prisoners, to lift the five men from their feet, all groaning in agony as their body weight pulls on their shoulders once their feet leave the ground. Miguel's hands are in the air, while Marcos's are straight out. Vibora grabs Marcos' left hand, ordering his men.

Vibora:

Raise their backs. I want them to see this.

Marcos cries as Sonrisa and Steve can now see this maniac with their youngest son's finger between the shears.

Sonrisa:

YOU FUCKING COWARD!!!

Mi Latina

Vibora:

You two better not look away, or I will kill these little bastards!

Two of Vibora's men go and hold STEVE and Sonrisa's heads toward Vibora.

Sonrisa:

(to Steve) Tell him where those girls are, Steve!!! (yelling to Marcos) It's going to be okay, mi amor. Daddy's going to save you.

Steve:

They're at the hotel. 134, 135, 136.

Vibora:

Now, was that so hard?

Vibora applies pressure to the shears, causing Marcos to scream out in pain. Sonrisa cries loudly, for her and her son. Steve yells.

Steve:

I'LL KILL YOU, YOU FUCKING SNAKE!!!

Marcos's pinky finger falls to the floor. Vibora applies pressure to the ring finger, clipping it, using force, ignoring Sonrisa's cries, Steve's threats and Miguel and Marcos' tears. After the ring finger hits the floor, Vibors clips the middle finger. Marcos vomits from the pain and crying. Vibora sees this and stops cutting fingers. He takes a box cutter from inside his jacket pocket, and runs it across Marcos' throat.

Vibora:

I was tired of him screaming. I just told you, vipers bite kids.

Sonrisa screams so hard that it's silent, her mouth wide, eyes closed, tears flowing. Vibora's men release Sonrisa and Steve, watching in horror as Vibora frees Marcos' wrists from their restraints, grabs the two-year-old's corpse by the collar of his shirt, and tosses him like a rag doll into the cage with the four starving pit bulls, who immediately begin to devour Marcos.

Steve:

YOU NO-GOOD SON-OF-A-BITCH!!!!

Vibora, ignoring him, approaches Miguel, and slices his throat with the box cutter.

Steve cries as Miguel looks into his eyes with that look of utter terror as he bleeds out. Sonrisa's wail makes Steve close his eyes. Nothing he has ever done or been through could've ever prepared him for this living nightmare.

Vibora reaches up, cutting the string that holds Miguel's hands up, dragging his body to the cage, lifts, and tosses it in, causing two of the dogs to rush it, immediately tearing into it's flesh, through the clothes.

Vibora pulls a .44 automatic from his waist as he walks to the wall, presses a button that lowers the five dangling men. Once they're to their knees, Vibora walks down the line, putting one bullet between each man's eyes.

Vibora signals to his men. The closest one to Sonrisa wheels a tank of gas with a gas mask attached to it, next to her bed, places the mask over her face, turns the nozzle, causing a hiss to fill the room. A few seconds later, Sonrisa begins to drift into a deep sleep.

The next man wheels an identical tank next to Steve, but, Vibora does the honors.

Vibora:

When you first came here, I told you, 'Welcome to Colombia,' but, now, allow me to—

The last thing Steve sees is the mask covering his face as the gas tank hisses that horrible sound.

Vibora:

—welcome you to Mi Casa.

FADE TO BLACK

PART 2 ENDS

# Part 3:
# The Ugly

## ACT 8: SCENE 27-11 A.M. - THE NEXT DAY

The black screen becomes faded as blurred light appears and goes black again. Grunting is heard, and Steve's vision becomes clearer as he wipes his eyes.

The first thing he notices is that the restraints that held him to the bed are undone. Next, he looks up and around, visual flashes of his sons' torture, then deaths; then he sees his five accomplices' murders, and can only duck his head into his right hand in shame. He looks to where all seven bodies hung, realizing there's no trace of evidence that any crime has taken place here. No blood on the floor, no brain matter, no body parts. Nothing! He looks at the dog cage and only sees the animals as they lie on the floor, obviously satisfied after consuming his son's corpses.

He looks down, eyes bulging at the sight of the red stain between his legs. He reaches down, feeling only an inch worth of penis, no testicles, and vomits. Next, he undoes his button and zipper, taking a peek at gauze taped where his scrotum used to be, and holds his brand-new thumb-sized penis, and vomits again. He takes a few deep breaths, then buttons and zips his pants back up.

He looks at his unconscious wife, and spots blood on the midsection of her shirt and waistline, immediately coming to the conclusion that, if they wrecked her vagina, they had to remove what would've been a very small fetus that was present in the womb. He puts his head into his palms.

Fade to black.

Heading: 'While They Were Sleeping' appears on the screen.

Vibora places the mask onto Steve's face, saying…

Vibora:

Welcome you to Mi Casa.

Vibora watches as Steve slips into unconsciousness.

One of his men speaks into a walkie-talkie, and, after a few seconds pass, four people in white coats and surgical masks walk down the stairs, strapping on surgical gloves.

The two men that assisted in the gassing of Sonrisa and Steve, open a drawer, turn on a few machines that beep a few times as they come to life; such as, a heart monitor, blood pressure and pulse reader, as the men place the attachments onto their patients. After this is done, the beeping steadies as Steve and Sonrisa's vitals are registered by the machines.

Behind them, the rest of the men take down the five cadavers and hose their blood and brains down a drain in the corner of the room.

A man walks up to the dog cage, watching the starving beasts eat the children. One of the dogs looks at him and growls menacingly, signalling that they are far from done with their meal.

Another man looks over his shoulder.

Male:

Fucking shame!

They both return to assist with the removal of the five dead men.

At the operating table, the two "doctors" that hover over Sonrisa remove her clitoris with a scalpel, handing it back to Vibora, who says…

Vibora:

So pretty. (He holds it up.) I would lick it, but, fortunately, I know where it's been.

All laugh.

The surgeon with the scalpel reaches into Sonrisa.

Surgeon:

There's something in here. I think she may be pregnant.

Vibora

Not anymore. Take it, and her tubes and ovaries as well.

Vibora turns to Steve's table, where another surgeon hands Vibora Steve's testicles.

Vibora:

I should probably make some dice out of these. Might be lucky. (He points at the now smooth spot.) Cauterize that. The least we could do for him is make sure it's clean and smooth, like his bald head.

Laughter.

The surgeon places the scalpel on the base of Steve's penis.

Vibora:

NO!! ( He holds up his thumb.) Leave this much. A man should at least have something to piss with.

The surgeon slices, handing it to Vibora, who tosses it into the dog cage. The dog it hits, turns, and eats it, immediately returning to the torso of Marcos, resuming his main course.

The surgeon who operates on Sonrisa removes the four-month-old fetus from a hole that was cut up to her navel, holding it chest high, as it moves slightly, dripping blood and fluid. Vibora takes it, walks it to the dogs, tosses it in to the animals, who make quick work of the tiny meal, only to return to the bigger dishes.

Vibora walks to the sinks, washes his hands thoroughly, and makes his way back to the tables.

He watches as a surgeon cauterizes Steve's scrotal wound with a sizzle, and Sonrisa's surgeon expertly sew her now destroyed stomach and vaginal area, back together.

Vibora:

Make sure everything is cleaned before bandaging. The least we can do is make sure they don't die from infection.

Three men, one with a hose, watch as the dogs step away from what used to be Miguel and Marcos, that are now only bare ribcages with shredded clothes attached. Two of the men open the cage, each one retrieves a body, and makes their exit. The man with the hose sprays the animals faces, causing them to lap water. He then aims the hose at the blood stains, sending them down a drain that rests in the center of the cage.

Flash to Real-Time: Steve looks at the four sleeping dogs in the now clean cage, and turns left, looking at Sonrisa, dreading what he must now do. He stands gingerly, favoring his fresh crotch wounds, and makes his way to his wife.

Meanwhile: Roockie-Sigue Bailando Mi Amor plays throughout the scene as Anita holds Anabella, who sits in her lap, both crying, as Anita leans into Paulo. They sit under their family portrait.

Paulo:

Mi amores, we have to go now. If they came and took your parents, they most certainly will come back for you two.

Anita:

I just want to stay here and die.

Anabella:

(crying, reaching up, drying Anita's tears) Don't say that, hermana. Are you going to leave me all alone, again?!

Anita:

(starts crying harder, drying Anabella's tears) No, hermanita, never. I'm just so sad for our family, and scared. I'll never leave you. We might be all that we have now. Anita and Anabella Jerez-Davis. We're family, now, blood.

She kisses Anabella's forehead, and Anabella lays her head on Anita's chest.

Meanwhile: Three black vans speed into the hotel parking lot. A three-way screen of the hotel rooms appears, six girls in one room, five in each of the remaining two, all share two beds, and are scared awake as the doors are kicked open simultaneously.

In the lobby, one of the bandits hands the clerk a wad of money.

The girls are all marched out of the hotel and down the stairs at gunpoint with assault rifles.

Meanwhile: Steve shakes Sonrisa awake. She grunts in pain as she sits up, with Steve's assistance, and places her hands on her stomach, looking at Steve's blood-stained midsection, and realizing that, not only did Vibora steal her unborn child from her womb, he took her womb as well.

Sonrisa:

(screams and cries out) NOOOOOOOOO!!! HE TOOK OUR BABY!!! HE KILLED OUR CHILDREN!!! HE KILLED OUR BOYS!!! MY BOYS!!! OUR BABY!!!

Steve reaches out and tries, in vain, to comfort his grieving wife, but she pushes him away, crying loudly the entire time.

Sonrisa:

He mangled us, Diablo! HE MANGLED US AND MURDERED OUR BOYS!!! ( She rises as fast as her fresh surgical wounds will allow, and slaps Steve with each hand numerous times, crying harder with each blow she delivers.) It's all your fault, DIABLO!!! IT'S ALL YOUR FAULT!!!

She leans into Steve's chest, crying as he holds her.

Sonrisa:

He took our child out of me and fed Marcos and Miguel to those animals. (She looks at the dog cage, screaming) ANIMALS!!!

Steve turns her away from the dogs as she continues to weep into his chest.

Steve:

The girls are with Paulo, angelita. They're safe. We have to go to them, now.

Sonrisa:

Yes, yes. Our girls. We have to go to them now, mi diablo. We have to protect them now.

They both look at the staircase, aghast.

Sonrisa:

Do we just leave, mi marido?!

Steve:

That's what I plan to do. The way I see it, if he wanted us dead, we'd be dead. If he wanted to torture us further, we'd still be strapped to those beds. Believe me, in his own sadistic way, him taking our genitals, and killing...he feels as if he's done enough.

He dries her eyes and they exchange a few quick pecks.

Steve:

I'm so sorry, mi amor. I love you and I apologize for all of this. I know I can never apologize enough for this.

Sonrisa:

( looking at Steve with tears welling up in her eyes, which are full of empathy) Mi Diablito, I love you, so much, mi amor. And, this isn't completely your fault. Vibora has been tormenting me since I was born. He's a monster. He was a monster before you came here, and he's still a monster. You're the only man that I have, or ever will, love. You're mi vengador (my avenger). No man has ever tried to defend my honor. Ever! Until you, mi rezo (my prayer), Mi Diablito, came to me. I love you. An Angel prayed to God and got a Devil.

They smile at one another, touch foreheads, and kiss. Steve kisses her head and nods toward the staircase.

Steve:

Let's get this over with.

Sonrisa places her hand in his, they squeeze, and Steve leads the way.

Meanwhile: 12:13 P.M.: At their house, Anita is oblivious to Paulo hitting a series of buttons on his phone, then placing it into his pocket.

Paulo:

Anita, we need to get you two out of here. I can't protect you two without a gun, and can only do so much alone.

Anita:

I don't want to leave, yet.

Paulo:

You'll never want to leave. It's your home. But, until we either get word on what happened, or let time pass, it's not safe.

Anita rubs Anabella's face and looks Paulo in the eyes.

Anita:

I have to take care of my little sister. Where will we go?

Paulo:

With me and my mother. She'll love having some women in the house with her to gang up on me.

Paulo smiles as Anita grins weakly.

Anita:

Let's go pack.

Meanwhile: 12:30 P.M.: Steve and Sonrisa push the door open as they climb the last step, and notice movement in the living room to their left, hearing faint conversation and laughter. Sonrisa gets scared, squeezes Steve's hand, and leans closer to him.

Sonrisa:

They're going to kill us, papi.

Steve:

SHHHH, calm down, mi angelita. Don't cry, and don't let them see you

261

nervous. Be strong. I'm here. And, whatever you do, don't fall for their taunting.

He kisses her, and they walk. Upon turning left, they spot five men, two smoke cigarettes, all are drunk and drinking from three open bottles of tequila. They look at Steve and Sonrisa blankly, as the lovers look at them, left to right.

Steve:

Gentlemen.

Steve walks to the table, picks up a pack of cigarettes, takes one out, puts it into his mouth, and lights it. He places the pack into his left pocket, along with a lighter, and picks up the tequila bottle with the most alcohol in it, and takes a swig, saying...

Steve:

You fellas don't mind if the wife and I take this, do you? I mean, we did just have to watch our boys get slaughtered, and had our genitals removed.

A man nods in the affirmative, as one of his friends says...

Male:

You two have fun fucking, now.

The five men laugh heartily at this. Steve stares at him blankly, takes another gulp from the bottle as Sonrisa nudges him toward the door, and says...

Steve:

Your boss may have taken my nuts, but, he didn't take my balls.

Four men, with the exception of the one who spoke to Steve, laugh uproariously. Sonrisa pushes Steve, and he responds by moving toward the door.

Vibora stands at his window, looking down on his front yard, and notices Steve and Sonrisa as they walk, side by side, Steve with the tequila bottle in his left hand, right arm around Sonrisa's shoulders; Sonrisa with her left arm around his waist.

The six men who guard the gate, watch them approach quizzically, looking at their blood-stained clothing.

Vibora sees Steve and Sonrisa getting closer to the gate, reaches to a panel on the wall to his right, presses a button, and the gate opens.

Steve and Sonrisa never stop their strides as the gate opens, nodding at the armed guards as they make their way down the dirt road that leads to and from the property.

Scene 28-12:45 P.M.: Piso 21 ft. Nicky Jam-Suele Suceder plays throughout the scene as the montage footage rotates left, alternating shots of the following:

Paulo and Anita fold and pack clothes while Anabella is piggy-backed onto Paulo, with her legs on his hips, and her arms around his neck. Anita looks at them and smiles from across the bed.

12:57 P.M.: Steve and Sonrisa walk down a road with jungle on either side of them, when they spot a churro stand, and six small children, all begging the vendor. Sonrisa looks at this scene sadly, holding her clutched hands to her bosom, aching for the poor children. She bats her eyes at Steve, who swigs from the tequila bottle, pats his pockets, and his eyes widen as he feels money he didn't expect to find. Sonrisa smiles brightly, takes the money, and walks across the street to the churro vendor with Steve in tow. The children notice the vendor staring behind them at the strange woman with a handful of American dollars, being followed by a black American man, and get excited at the prospect of receiving the treat that they were just begging for.

Sonrisa picks up the smallest of the bunch, a boy in a diaper and a T-shirt, kisses his cheek, peels off a bill, hands it to the vendor, and, churros all around. Sonrisa tickles the baby she holds as he stuffs his face and laughs. She catches Steve smiling at her, she returns the gesture.

1:08 P.M.: Anita, Paulo, and Anabella sit at the table in the kitchen, eating sandwiches, chips, cookies and drinking juice.

1:10 P.M.: Steve and Sonrisa cross an intersection, minus the tequila bottle.

1:20 P.M.: Paulo carries two bags, while Anita carries one, and holds Anabella's hand with her free one, as they walk toward the end of her block. They turn right, and, two men jump out of a gray van, armed with assault rifles, pointing them at Anita and Anabella, while a third man approaches Paulo with a brown paper bag, handing it to him, and shaking his hand. Anita looks at Paulo, horrified at this betrayal, and screams at him.

Anita:

PAULO, WHAT'RE YOU DOING, YOU FUCKING FAGGOT!!! MALDITO!!! MY FATHER WAS RIGHT!!! HE SHOULD'VE CUT YOUR FUCKING BALLS OFF!!! I LOVED YOU!!! I TRUSTED YOU!!! AFTER EVERYTHING I'VE BEEN THROUGH!!!

She spits angrily in his direction as the men grab her and Anabella. The last thing she sees through tear-soaked eyes is Paulo pulling at least three bundles of money from the brown paper bag, smiling at the man who paid him. The men throw her into the van, followed by Anabella, who hurries to her. They both cry, yet again, as Anabella sits on Anita's lap, Anita rocking back and forth, stroking Anabella's hair, staring angrily at her captors. The last man enters the van, shuts the door, and the van proceeds forward, driving down her block.

1:22 P.M.: At that instance, Steve and Sonrisa come upon their corner, looking at, but sensing nothing strange about the gray van as they stop to let it drive by them. Once it passes, Steve and Sonrisa get hopeful eyes as they see their humble abode. They move as fast as their wounded midsections will allow.

Inside the house, the front door opens, and Sonrisa calls her daughter's names as she walks to their bedroom, finding nothing. Steve walks into the kitchen, noticing three cups and plates on the table, and walks down the hall to where his wife cries.

He stops just outside of the boy's room, dropping his head, as ( a vision of a screaming Marcos slams through his mind, and both of Marcos's fingers hit the floor, with two loud thuds that echo in his brain. Show Marcos and Miguel getting their throats slit, then show Vibora tossing their bodies into the dog cage, and the animals immediately ravaging them).

Steve charges into the room, picks up a screaming Sonrisa, who struggles so hard, Steve drops her to the floor, and pulls her from the boy's room by her right arm. Once outside of the room, he shuts the door, and commences to drag her, kicking and screaming, crying on the way to the living room couch. He sits, placing both of his forearms under her armpits, and lifts her into his lap, where she places her head onto his shoulder, and cries her eyes out, yet again, a mother, mourning the deaths of her sons. The camera pans back, showing them in this embrace, under the family portrait.

Fade to Black

Act 9-Scene 29: The Next Day-8:43 A.M.

The same man who paid off the hotel desk clerk, when his men rounded up the sixteen ladies from the three hotel rooms, now escorts Anita, who carries a sleeping Anabella, down a poorly lit tunnel, accompanied by three other men.

Anita:

Where're you taking me and my sister? We're hungry, if you care.

The four men ignore her as the lead man stops abruptly, removes a set of keys from his pocket, and begins fiddling with a lock. It clicks open, the leader opens the door, which creaks loudly, revealing the sixteen ladies, who all look at the door, not knowing what to expect, and see Anita holding Anabella.

Anita looks at the women, mortified, and is shoved into the room with them. The door slams shut. Anita looks around nervously as one of the girls that lay on one of the four mattresses, gets up and motions for Anita to sit Anabella down. Anita walks toward the mattress, lays a squirming Anabella onto it, where she is greeted with a blanket by one of the other captives. One of them asks…

Female #1:

What're your names?

Anita:

I'm Anita, and, this is my sister, Anabella.

Fem. #2:

The swine are even taking babies, now!

Anita:

What is this? And, where're they taking us?

Fem. #3:

This is the sex trade. We don't know where they're taking us, but, we'll know when we get there.

Fem. #4:

One thing is for sure. We're all whores now.

A chorus of disapproval is heard momentarily.

Anita:

(thinking to herself, but it's audible) Mamita did it to feed me and Miggy and Marcos. If she could do it for us, I can do it for Anabella. ( She actually says) How did you all end up here?

Fem. #5:

It was crazy. We all come from different places. Next thing you know, we get off a boat, and they put us all on a truck. A little while later, gunshots…

Fem. #3:

…then, the door slides open a few minutes later, and a black American and three or four other men tell us that we were free, and that they would send us home and not touch us.

Anita:

That black American was our father!

A collective gasp of speculation from the rest.

Fem. #2:

No, you two aren't black!

Anita:

He married our mother.

Fem. #4:

Anyway, your papa turns around, jumps out of the truck, and murdered five men that were probably driving as security.

Fem. #1:

How'd you two end up here?

Anita:

(scowling at the memory) Mi novio Paulo sold me to these bastards! My sister just happened to be with me.

Fem. #2

Why did your father shoot those men and set us free?

Anita:

It's a long story.

Fem. #3:

We have nothing but time, amiga.

Anita:

Have you ever heard of Vibora?

The girls all murmur and scuttle about from excitement.

Fem. #4:

Who hasn't?!

Anita:

Well, he made my mother a prostitute at twelve because her father stole some drugs from his father. At twenty-one, he let her go. This past April, she met my father, Steve, the black American. They got married on my fifteenth birthday, and their wedding reception was also my Quinceañera. It was such a big party, me and my siblings had so much fun. Then, one night, last month, Steve was in Vibora's car, told my mother that Vibora said something disrespectful about her, and he killed his bodyguards. Now, two days ago, my little brothers were kidnapped. Me, Anabella, and my ex-boyfriend Paulo got away. Yesterday, I went home, and my parents were gone. (crying now, as Anabella walks to her, holding her hand) Now, here we are.

A few ladies wipe away tears.

Fem. #7:

It sounds so much like a novel. So romantic, yet, so tragic.

Fem. #4:

I wish a man would start a war over me!

Anabella:

( tugging at Anita's hand, looking around nervously) Anita, where are we? I'm hungry. Did Daddy start a war over Mama?

Anita:

(picking up Anabella) Yes, hermana. Yes, he did.

The girls all move into a group embrace.

Fade to Black

Scene 30-July 27, 2009, 7:03 A.M.

S.O.N.Y.K.-La Mujer De Mi Suenos plays as an overhead shot shows Steve and Sonrisa sleeping face to face, holding each other, while her left leg is thrown over his right hip. Steve wakes up first and brushes her hair out of her face, causing her to stir. He touches her face gently, making her moan and scoot closer to him. He uses the tips of fingers, and lightly, yet audibly taps forehead, waking her up. She shows a slight irritation at this and straddles him, choking him playfully.

Sonrisa:

What's your problem, Diablito?

Steve:

I was trying to wake you up, sweetly at first, but, you know how you Latinas are. Y'all don't respond unless somebody goes upside y'all head.

He taps the side of her head, making a slapping sound with his mouth. Feigning shock, she smiles down at him, squeezing his neck a little harder, giggling as he turns and is now on top of her.

Sonrisa:

Maldito, get off of me!

Steve:

I'm about to give you your anniversary gift. Open your legs.

Sonrisa:

Aye, papi, I hope it's big.

Steve:

( reaching between his legs) Oh, it's big, and hard, too.

Sonrisa:

That's how I like them, Mi Diablito.

Steve:

( feigning surprise, looking at Sonrisa suspiciously) What did you do with it? Thief! My own wife, and on our anniversary.

Sonrisa laughs and pulls him down to her for a kiss.

Sonrisa:

Happy Anniversary, mi amor.

Steve:

Happy Anniversary, angelita.

They kiss. She tears up a little.

Steve:

Happy Birthday, 'Nita.

Sonrisa:

Happy Birthday, mi hija. (wiping tears before they can fall) She was so happy last year. She thought her birthday would just be us four, giving her gifts, something small. Then you come, Mi Diablito, Mi Heroe, and made me and her the happiest women in the world this day, one year ago. Te amo, papi.

Steve:

I love you, too.

Sonrisa:

What do you think she's doing, right now, mi amor?

Steve:

I don't know, but, I'm sure she's happy.

Meanwhile: 7:54 A.M: Madrid, Spain.

The sixteen ladies, plus Anabella, all gather around Anita, who sleeps in a bottom bunk, and sing Happy Birthday to her, while holding a cake with one candle on it. Anabella wakes her with a shove of her left arm.

Anabella:

Happy Birthday, hermana.

Anita:

(sitting up and stretching with a smile on her face, as she sees the cake, hugging Anabella) Thank you, hermanita. Thank you, mis amigas. ( She blows the candle out.)

Anabella:

How do you feel?

Anita:

For some strange a reason, I feel good.

Meanwhile: 10:37 A.M: Steve and Sonrisa, dressed in their wedding garb, exit a bank, descending its staircase, attracting attention from on-lookers, who think they were just married. They stop and wave at the people, who applaud and yell...

Crowd:

BESO, BESO, BESO!!!

They share a deep kiss, to the enjoyment of the crown as they clap and holler in celebration. Steve and Sonrisa wave at them as they make their way to their taxi.

Smash cut to them exiting the cab on an unidentified road. The cab driver pops the trunk as Steve hands him what looks to be at least $5-6 thousand dollars in a neatly rolled bundle.

Driver:

Gracias, Americano!!!

Steve:

You didn't hit any potholes.

All three laugh at this, and Steve and Sonrisa exit the vehicle. Steve goes to the trunk, lifts two duffel bags from it with a slight grunt, and steps to the side, allowing the taxi to turn, and go the way he came. Steve kneels and opens the bags, then extracts a beats-by-Dre speaker from it, and looks at his grinning wife-.

Sonrisa:

Diablo!

They share a smile.

Steve:

May I have this dance? What kind of husband doesn't dance with his wife on their anniversary?

Sonrisa:

Si.

Steve:

(teasing her, making a circle between them with his forefingers) Because, I want to dance with the prettiest Latina (looking around) in this general area, you know? I mean, between the two of us, you know, you're the prettiest Latina.

He laughs as she smiles and playfully attacks him with a barrage of slaps to the arms.

Sonrisa:

Diablo!

Steve retreats and goes to the speaker, presses a button, and Joey Montana-Amor Del Bueno plays in its entirety as they start dancing, holding one another, then separating as the song proceeds, doing their own solo moves, to each other's amusement. They hold each other as the song ends, and kiss.

Sonrisa:

Happy anniversary, Mi Diablito. I love you, so much.

Steve:

I love you, too, mi angelita. Happy anniversary. You ready to do this?

Sonrisa:

Si, mi amor.

Rapid montage footage rolls to the tune of Yandel-Plakito, as Sonrisa and Steve both sling assault rifle belt clips around their shoulders, four apiece; then reaching down, Sonrisa picks up an M-16, then bends, grabbing an AR-15, doing the same.

Steve places a .9mm with an extended clip into a holster strapped around his left shoulder, placing an identical weapon into a holster on his right shoulder. He reaches into a bag and comes up with an AK-47, which he places a bullet into from one of the belt clips, reaching into the bag again, bringing an M-16 with him.

Steve:

(placing a bullet into the M-16's chamber, speaking to Sonrisa) You got those guns strapped to your thighs, don't you? You know I like that, it's sexy.

Sonrisa:

( smiling shyly at him) Yes, papi, my thighs are loaded.

They smile at one another.

Steve:

Can I see for myself? *(He looks at her suspiciously.) It's not that I don't trust you or believe you, I just want to put my hand up your dress.

Sonrisa:

(grinning at him) Diablo, always trying to seduce pretty women.

Steve:

My work is never done. (He grins and winks at her. She smiles.)

Steve approaches Sonrisa, who faces him, holding her assault rifles up. He puts his assault rifles down, and, on his way up, rubs her thighs until he touches a gun.

Steve:

Is that a .9mm, or are you just happy to see me?

Sonrisa:

It's a .9mm.

Steve:

(laughing at his wife's joke.) Kitty got claws.

They share a kiss. Steve reaches into his back pocket and pulls his wallet out, flips it open, and looks at a wallet sized photo of their family portrait.

Sonrisa:

What're you looking at, papi?

Steve:

I think you know the answer to that.

He hands her the wallet, closes his eyes, bracing. Three seconds later, he hears her crying.

Steve:

Angelita, I need you to take that, and kill with it.

Sonrisa:

You're right, mi amor. ( She straightens, dries her eyes, and hands him his wallet back.) He killed our ninos.

Steve:

And, how are we going to pay him back?

Sonrisa:

By killing him.

Steve retrieves his assault rifles, and the couple starts their march toward the mansion. (The camera pans 180 degrees, showing Vibora's mansion.)

Alejandro Sanz-No Me Compares plays as they walk toward the mansion, up until they reach the gate.

Sonrisa:

I have something to tell you before we do this, mi amor.

Steve:

Now would be the time.

Sonrisa:

The night you got shot, Vibora sent five men to rape me and 'Nita. I come to this conclusion, because, they came right after you left, and four of them raped me and 'Nita in front of Paulo, Miguel, and Marcos.

Steve's eyes narrow as he takes all of this in.

Sonrisa:

Jesus, he was the vilest. He wore a white silk shirt—

Steve:

—And a cowboy hat?

Sonrisa:

( looking at him, stunned) How'd you know?

Steve:

He and his four buddies were escorting those girls Vibora asked about. And, for some unexplainable reason, I was so overcome with the urge to kill them, that I got a nosebleed. I shot all five of them. And, I really felt the urge when the one in the white silk shirt looked me in the eyes.

One of the guards notices the couple approaching the gate, still a ways off but getting closer. He beckons one of the other guards toward him. The second guard has binoculars around his neck, which he uses, and sees Steve and Sonrisa, armed. He pulls a walkie-talkie from his back pocket, presses a button and speaks…

Vibora hears the static-crackled voice say…

Guard:

It's the whore and the nigger, boss.

Vibora hits the button, opening the gate.

Vibora:

Come in. If they want a war, let's give it to them.

Steve and Sonrisa continue their conversation-

Sonrisa:

Now, remember, you take the right staircase, I'll go left. His mansion is literally two different houses. Bordello on the left, business on the right.

Steve:

I got it. And, at the end of both paths is his office.

Sonrisa:

Right. So, God forbid any mishaps, we should both meet each other right in front of his office.

Steve:

Tell me something, mi esposa?

Sonrisa:

Anything, mi amor.

Steve:

How does it feel to be the motivating force behind this war?

Sonrisa:

I don't think of it like that. I think of it in terms of, you were willing to do this for me, because, the cost we paid was too high. No matter what he put me through, Miguel and Marcos didn't deserve to die. And, our daughters don't belong out there, all alone, just to be orphaned, all over again. But, it feels wonderful, to experience what it feels like to have an avenger. Be careful what you wish for. When I prayed, I only wanted a good man, true love, and a family. What I got was what I asked for, and so much more. The only thing I'd change is what happened to our sons. Other than that, if putting my life on the line, after all that Vibora has put me through, is the only way I can balance the scale, so be it. He cheated me out of my first family and a childhood, he won't get away with cheating me out of my own family.

Sonrisa stares blankly at Vibora's mansion, while Steve looks at her with admiration.

Sonrisa:

Can I ask you something, Mi Diablito?

Steve:

Anything, mi amor.

Sonrisa:

After everything we've been through, do you believe in God, now?

Steve:

No.

Sonrisa:

( looking at him, somewhat disappointed) Why not, mi vengador?

Steve:

I told you that I'm a realist. And, all I can say for sure, is this; all of my child-hood, being told to read the Bible or Quran, to pray to this or that, to be-lieve this or that, never even came close to setting a fire inside of me the way you did, when I first laid eyes on you. All I did was look at you, and I be-lieved that, for whatever reason, you were mine. I touched you, I know this will sound cliché, and, I know you felt it, too, because you jumped a little, but, I felt the spark in my heart. It woke my insides up in a way religion never could. So, in summary, I guess what I'm trying to say, is that, I believe in you.

She has tears running down her cheeks when she walks up to him, and kisses him deeply.

Vibora watches this, slowly angering himself, not only at their love, but at the fact that, they still have the gall to challenge him.

Vibora:

Goddamn whore and her nigger!

The couple ends their kiss with a few pecks and walks to the open gate, studying the mansion momentarily.

Steve:

Looks like we were expected.

They walk toward an open front door, guns raised in unison.

Steve:

Remember the day we fought?

Sonrisa:

I remember every day that we spent together.

Steve:

There was a specific reason why I didn't violate you.

Sonrisa:

Because you love me.

Steve:

It was more than that. Come to find out, you and 'Nita were raped in front of the boys, but, right before I penetrated you, I heard your pleas for me to stop, and, I can swear I saw your face when you were fifteen, begging me, your husband, not to do that to you. Not only could I not do such a thing to my wife, I most definitely couldn't do it to a fifteen-year-old girl, or any woman for that matter. One thing for sure, I'd never become that in your eyes. Never!

Sonrisa:

You can't keep saying things like that, mi amor. We're on a mission.

Steve:

I know, I just thought you should know that.

They approach the door, sharing one last kiss before entering.

Sonrisa:

I love you, Mi Diablito.

Steve:

I love you, mi angelita.

Sonrisa:

For our children.

Steve:

For our children...and you.

They turn, putting their backs together, guns raised, and enter the house. They both fire their weapons simultaneously, noticing armed men as soon as they enter. Sonrisa mows down five men, Steve sprays four. They both walk

carefully, checking for more men. Both of them stand in front of their as-
signed staircases. Steve turns, noticing movement at the top of the staircase,
and sprays his weapons at two men, killing them instantly, just as Sonrisa
turns and notices a man behind Steve.

Sonrisa:

Move, Steve!

Steve runs up the staircase and Sonrisa squeezes the trigger, pumping four of
six rounds into the man's upper chest and throat, as one bullet takes his ear
off, and the other goes errant, striking a portrait of Vibora between the
Eyes. Sonrisa smiles at this.

Steve gets up, putting his hat back on, and smiles at his wife.

Steve:

Shall we? (He looks up the stairs.)

Sonrisa:

We shall.

They both walk up the staircase sideways, looking left to right, as they pro-
ceed. Once at the top, they peck lips one last time.

Sonrisa:

Be careful, Mi Diablito.

Steve:

You too, mi Angelita.

Scene 31: They place their backs together, and slide into the hallway. The camera swings, following Sonrisa, as gunfire is heard behind her. Shakira-Rabiosa plays throughout the scene.

In this hallway, there are two doors on either side of Sonrisa, and a right turn at the end. The first door on her left opens, and a man leaps out, to his death, as three shots from his handgun stray, and Sonrisa's shots hit him first in his head, then his chest. She steps to her right, side-stepping gingerly looking at the open door, and, seeing nothing, hurries past them. A three-way screen shows two men with guns behind the door on her left, and 3 men with assorted weapons, behind the doors on her right, all eight men watch the shadow that her feet cast as she makes her way past the door.

She walks backwards, facing the way she just came after she hears a door creak open. She raises her guns, hearing faint whispering and another door opening, then a third. She sees the first of three men and starts shooting both weapons. Just as those three are taking numerous bullets, Sonrisa turns as she hears a door open behind her. She turns, facing the new corpses, and hears gunfire down the hall, followed by five heavy thuds. She peers down the hallway, seeing five more dead men that she didn't kill, and notices Steve looking at her, tipping his hat with the barrel of his gun, and goes down a hall that's to her left, firing his weapons as he proceeds.

Sonrisa turns and immediately fires upon seeing flashes and hearing five shots, she hits the man seven times in his upper body, sending him lumbering backward until he hits the floor. Once he falls, she notices two holes, one in her upper left arm, the other in her left side.

Sonrisa:

( cursing herself) Sonrisa, you dumb bitch! You heard that door open.

She sees a leg step out and unleashes both weapons, sending bullets into the corner of the wall and door, sending splinters everywhere. She hears a feminine scream and runs to the doorway, seeing...

Sonrisa:

Tessa!

...sprawled on the floor, left thigh bleeding, along with several holes in her side, as she vainly applies pressure to a gaping hole that oozes blood from her jugular vein, coughing up blood, dressed only in panties.

Sonrisa:

( kneeling down, looking at her old friend) I'm so sorry, Tessa.

Tessa stops breathing, and Sonrisa is immediately on her feet, back in kill mode. ( Slo-mo shows the Bloody Bride, assault rifles raised, alternately firing them, and bodies dropping after her series of shots are delivered. Shakira Rabiosa, get louder.)

Seven bodies have dropped, as both of her weapons empty. She reloads with celerity, aggressively snatching the slides back on the weapons. She grimaces a bit, raising the weapon with her left hand, but hefts the weapon in her right hand with ease. She turns toward the semi-dark staircase that leads to Vibora's office, hearing footsteps, takes a deep breath, aims...

Scene 32-The scene rewinds showing every frame slightly faster than it actually happened, until she and Steve are at the top of the staircases.

Sonrisa:

Be careful, Mi Diablito.

Steve:

You too, mi Angelita.

They place their backs together, and slide into the hallway. The camera swings, following Steve, who immediately opens fire on eight armed men, mowing them down as he moves each weapon, expertly, from left to right. Don Omar ft. Fabolous-Dale Don Dale plays throughout the scene.

Five doors line this hallway, three on the left, two on the right. Steve aims each weapon in its respective direction, and doesn't have to wait long for two men to appear, running from the hall way on his left, the only turn available to him, shooting without aiming, as Steve fires both weapons, delivering all head and body shots with only three straying.

He cautiously steps on bodies while keeping his eyes on the doors, coming to the conclusion that they're empty once he gets in front of the last one. He turns left abruptly, aiming his weapons down a now-empty hallway, and, seeing shapes in his peripheral vision, turns, and, not seeing Sonrisa in Harm's Way, fires both weapons at the men as he hears her guns blazing and all eight bodies dropping after about fifteen seconds worth of gunshots.

He sees Sonrisa peek down the hallway at him, and touches the brim of his hat with the tip of his assault rifle barrel in his right hand, and turns right firing down the hallway at four men who get numerous shots off at him, but only land three, as Steve bombards them all with a barrage of bullets from two assault rifles that he swings from side to side, covering the entire area, watching bodies drop.

He examines his wounds. One in his upper left pectoral muscle, two in his gut.

The Bloody Groom stands up straight, feeling no pain, fueled by adrenaline, and fires at the three new victims who shoot, offering themselves willingly, in protection of their boss. They each catch a few headshots that knock chunks from their faces and scalps; as this time, not only does Steve have to quickly reload, he coughs up blood, noticing a fresh chest wound, dead center, in his heart. He reloads quickly, leaning up against the wall, taking deep breaths while snatching the slides back. He looks at the staircase that leads to Vibora's office, hearing footsteps, aims, and…

A split-screen shows Steve and Sonrisa, both aiming both weapons up their respective staircases, taking simultaneous deep breaths, and firing both weapons as they slowly approach their staircases. Flashes that can be from machine guns or handguns are visible in each staircase as the men open fire. Sonrisa catches four bullets; two in her breasts, one in her right shoulder, and the last in the middle of her gut. She falls to her right knee on the first step, uses the gun in her right hand as a makeshift crutch to hold her steady, aims the weapon in her left hand, and sprays until it's empty, breathing heavily as six dead men are first heard, then seen, tumbling down the stairs. Once the heaps are completed, she tosses the now useless M-16 to the side. She checks the belt clip to the AR-15, estimating around twenty shots, and reaches under her dress, where the snap of Velcro is heard, coming up with a .9mm. She coughs up blood, aggressively spitting it out in one big gob, wipes her mouth, narrows her eyebrows, and heads up the stairs, both guns raised.

Simultaneously: Steve aims and fires both of his weapons, ducking and dodging bullets as best as he can as he hears stray headshots whizzing by both of his ears. While shooting the somewhat dark staircase, a bullet grazes his bald scalp, leaving a blood trail an inch and a half long on the right, and, as he dips to his left, a bullet removes that ear completely. He stands up straight, eyes bulging in shock.

Steve:

SHIT!!!

He starts blasting away, and doesn't stop as three bodies roll and thud down the staircase. He feels two shots hit, both in his hip, but never stops firing, screaming out briefly as his AK-47 empties, the shots and gun flashes from the staircase cease as four more corpses tumble down the stairs as his M-16 empties.

Steve tosses the weapons, reaches behind his back with both hands, exposing both .9mm's with extended clips, as he removes them from their holsters, one black, the other chrome, Desert Eagles. Taking his staircase, in-sync with Sonrisa, who begins her ascension.

The split-screen is trifurcated by a third screen, showing Vibora seated in his office, calmly, at his desk, downing a shot of vodka, puffing on a Cuban cigar, and cocking two chrome AK-47's, facing the entrance to his office.

Vibora's screen descends from view, bringing the split-screen back, and, just as Steve and Sonrisa concurrently take the last step, the dividing line in the split-screen ascends from view, making it a full-screen as they smile at one another. Wesley Tones-De Cabeza plays throughout-

Steve:

( smiling at Sonrisa) Easy as 1-2-3.

Sonrisa:

You probably saved my life, or at least prolonged it.

Steve:

You're my wife. You ready?

Sonrisa:

Si, mi amor.

( Slo-mo)) Steve and Sonrisa turn toward Vibora's office, blasting away, and end up catching multiple shots as Vibora lets loose with his twin AK's, he catches an ample amount of body shots himself. Sonrisa fires, hitting Vibora in his right eye, sending a chunk of his brain from the exit wound, but she takes a bullet in her throat, one of Vibora's last shots. Steve drops to his knees, and shoots his last shot, which enters Vibora's mouth, sending yet another piece of his brain from a gaping exit wound in the base of his head. Steve takes Vibora's last shot to his heart, which knocks him to his back. ( Slo-mo ends.)

Steve notices Sonrisa holding the hole in her throat, in a futile effort to stop the flow of blood from the wound. Steve coughs up a gob of blood and crawls to his wife, who tilts her head toward him, smiling weakly as she dies. Steve leans on his left arm.

Steve:

We killed the Snake, angelita. We got him!

They both tear up as Steve places his forehead on hers. He leans to his right, coughs up blood, and lays his head on Sonrisa's stomach. He can hear her heartbeat as it slows down, along with his, and smiles to himself when Sonrisa's right hand falls onto his head. They take their final breaths together as an overhead shot shows Vibora's entire office, and the Bloody Bride and Groom's in-sync heartbeats become audible, getting louder, as they slow gradually until, at last, they die.

BOOM BOOM!!! BOOM…BOOM!!!

A flat-line beep is heard, as the scene fades to black.

Act 10-Scene 33, April 17, 2011, 2:27 P.M..: Madrid, Spain.

Chino & Nacho-Lo Que Tu No Sabes plays faintly, and gets louder, the closer the camera descends onto the club from its overhead view. Once an anonymous patron in a suit, holding a briefcase, enters the establishment, opening the door, the song booms as a mysteriously packed-in-the-afternoon night club is exposed, as are all of the women employees, as their breasts swing freely, be they waitress, or dancer.

The man with the briefcase asks a topless young woman bartender something in her ear as they lean over the bar, meeting each other halfway. She points to a young woman, who pole dances topless for six gentlemen. He hands the bartender a bill, she smiles, looking down on the American $50, as he makes his way toward the attractive young dancer.

The dancer turns her back to the camera. The camera is right on her ass as she starts to thumb down her thong.

Male:

Anita Jerez-Davis?

She turns around, shocked, as her small audience collectively voices their disappointment at this interruption. The man hands her a $100 dollar bill, asking...

Male:

Miss Jerez-Davis?

Anita:

( taking the money from his hand) Si.

Male:

I have to speak with you.

She holds up a finger, examines the bill, and looks at him.

Male:

It's urgent.

Anita apologizes to her audience as she puts her halter top back on, picks up her dollars that were thrown at her during her routine, and takes the man who wants to talk with her, hand, as he assists her down from the stage. Anita leads him down a hallway, with rooms with only stringed beads for doors, with women in them, either performing fellatio, or bent over, getting penetrated from the back, or straddling their johns. The man in the suit gets nervous.

Male:

( looking nervous) I didn't come here for this, Miss Jerez-Davis.

Anita:

(aggressively walking into his face) Then why did you come here, papi?! You do know what it is we do, here, don't you?!

Male:

Yes, but, trust me, what I have to show you, and give you and your little sister, could take you both out of this place.

Anita:

(grabbing his tie, angrily) How do you know about my little sister, papi! She's only eight years old! Is that what you're into, papi, pequenas?! Are you a pervert or something?

Male:

(holding his hands up in a mock surrender) I know exactly why you're protective of your little sister, and somewhat paranoid—

Anita:

Do you, do you? Did your boyfriend sell you to international sex-traffickers, right after your little brothers, mother, and father were kidnapped and more than likely slaughtered by a drug lord?!

Male:

No. And, I admit, I know the first half of that story, but had no idea that your boyfriend did this to you. I'm sorry.

Anita:

(tearing up and folding her arms in anger) It's okay. It's not your fault.

The man hands her a pure white handkerchief from his inside pocket.

Male:

Miss Colombiana, if I could speak with you and the Princesa in a quieter setting?

Anita:

(crying fully now) My father was the only one who's ever called us that.

Male:

Now you know that I come in peace.

She hugs him, apologizing repeatedly.

Anita:

I'm sorry, I'm so sorry, I didn't know, I've...we've been through so much... Mister...?

Santiago:

Santiago Santos, call me Santy.

Anita:

Right this way, Santy.

An eight-year-old Anabella lays flat on her stomach, with an open book on her left, looking at it, and writing it down, when the door creaks open, revealing her sister with a strange man accompanying her. She runs to Anita.

Anabella:

'Nita, who is this strange man? I thought you girls weren't allowed to bring men back here?

Anita and Santiago laugh as Anita bends to kiss her cheek.

Anita:

He's not a stranger, he's a friend of Papa's.

Anabella:

(disbelievingly) No, he's not?!

Santiago:

If I wasn't, would I know that you showed up on their doorstep one night, and, he said when you told him your name, was Anabella, all he heard was Princess?

Anabella:

( excited) Where's Mama and Papa and our brothers?!

Anita:

Calm down, Ana, that's what he's about to tell us.

They sit at a table, while Anabella stands between Anita's legs, while Anita holds her with both hands. Santiago opens his briefcase, pulling out a laptop, activates the machine, presses a series of keys, then turns the screen toward the ladies.

Santiago:

(to Anabella) Princess, if you would hit the return key, please?

Anita points to it, and Anabella presses it, and the screen instantly shows Steve, and Sonrisa sitting on his lap, dressed in their wedding uniforms. Anita and Anabella begin to cry as they rub their parents' crucifixes.

Shakira-Gitana plays.

Steve and Sonrisa:

Happy Birthday, 'Nita!

Anita:

(touches the screen) Happy Anniversary, Mama and Papa.

Steve:

Hopefully, Princess is with you, and, if so, even though we got separated, I kept my promise to you when I gave you my necklace, and your sister, your mother's, and told you that we'd be happy when you all came back. It's now ten months after that day, our first anniversary, and Miss Colombiana's sixteenth birthday. I don't know where, or if, this message, will ever find you, I've had Santy, here, put up certain digital roadblocks, hopefully, they'll work, but, I'm about to give you some closure in regards to the night Vibora kidnapped your brothers. There's no easy way to say this, but, he murdered them. 'Nita and Ana, the bastard murdered your brothers, and he took our child out of your mother's belly. Believe me, I don't want to say what he did, your mother doesn't want, or need, to hear it again, it was bad enough that she had to endure that. But the man is a monster.

Steve pauses momentarily to comfort his bawling wife.

Anita and Anabella comfort each other. Santy cries silently, watching the two-time orphaned sisters comfort each other. Santy reaches as if to pause the recording.

Anita:

Let it play, Santy. (Stroking Anabella's hair and drying her eyes, Anabella dries Anita's.) See how handsome Papa looked in his suit, and how beautiful Mama looked in her dress?

Anabella nods in agreement, Steve continues.

Steve:

'Nita, know this, we're going to pay Vibora a visit, today. We don't plan on making it back, but, we do plan to take Vibora with us. Revenge sounds like a wonderful anniversary gift slash birthday present, doesn't it?

Anita pauses the recording.

Anita:

(to Santiago) Did they kill him?

Santiago:

Yes.

Anita:

Are they dead? ( Tears leave her eyes, feeling that she knows the answer.)

Santiago:

Yes, that's why I'm here.

Anita:

(starting to grin maniacally) Was it bloody?

Santiago:

The paper said, and I quote, 'Vibora, Massacred by Bloody Bride and Groom.'

Anita smiles as she kisses Anabella's cheek, and restarts the message.

Steve:

And, once your brothers told us that you were safe with Paulo, we breathed little easier in that regard.

Now, 'Nita, I have to say this to you. When your mother and I first met, and she mentioned kids, I knew not to come in, trying too hard to form a false bond with you and Miguel. You two had already spent those years with your mother. Not to mention what I was up against, you going through what you went through, with two of your mother's previous men. So, I did the only thing that I could do, which was just be there, offer advice when needed, crack a few jokes, feed and clothe you all, try my absolute hardest to protect you. Basically, be a friend. And, hope for the best. Prove myself by not doing the vile things men have done to you in the past, and try to brighten your future, and show you all that, just because you were orphaned, doesn't mean that life is, or will always be, bad. And, even if you never think of me as a father, a real father, I hope you can at least look at my actions, and at the very least, consider me a friend.

Anita presses a button, pausing the recording, crying. Anabella wipes her tears away, making room for new ones.

Anabella:

He loved us, 'Nita.

Anita:

I know that now, hermanita. I know that, now.

She restarts the recording.

Steve:

(receiving a kiss on his cheek from his bride) I love you, 'Nita. I love my princess. ( Anabella laughs at the mention of her name.) I love mi angelita. (He turns and pecks Sonrisa's lips.) I love Miggy and Marcos. I didn't realize just how much until you all were put in harm's way. But, I love you all. I hope you two like your gifts.

Anita pauses the recording as Prince Royce-Las Cosas Pequenas plays.

Anita:

Gifts, what gifts?!

Santiago opens his briefcase, pulling out two jewelry boxes, and slides them across the table to the gasping ladies. They open the boxes, revealing two gold chains with charms, one reads 'Miss Colombiana' the other says 'Princesa.' Giddy with joy, they squeal and help each other put on yet another necklace from their parents. Anita restarts the recording.

Steve and Sonrisa:

Happy Birthday, 'Nita!

Steve:

I hope you and Ana like your gifts. Girls can never have too much jewelry.

And, use our last gift to you two, wisely. Your mother has something she wants to say. I love you, mis ninas.

Sonrisa:

I'll keep it short, mis hijas. 'Nita, Happy Birthday, mi amor. I remember the day we found each other. It made me so happy to help you. You were just as sweet and innocent as Anabella, and just like her, didn't deserve whatever made you two orphans. You were just babies. Miguel, too. So sweet and scared. All alone. I also remember our wedding day, and your Quinceañera. You and Steve looked so cute dancing together. He made us both the happiest women in the world on this day, one year ago. I wish so bad that every obstacle in our way would just vanish so that we could just be happy, and Steven could dance with Anabella on her fifteenth birthday, give you two ninas away at your weddings, and you two and the boys could've given us hundreds of nietos. But, that's not the hand we were dealt. We were dealt a bloody, fighting hand. From the day I was born, and Steve, it's always been a fight. Unfortunately, it had to spill over into our children's lives. But, him taking Miguel and Marcos from us was his last straw. Your father and I will make one last grand attempt to balance the scales. Hopefully, him putting his life on the line for your brothers and me, and you two girls, just in case Vibora has something to do with whatever you two may be going through, will convince you of his sincerity, 'Nita. We have to go, now. If princess is with you, kiss her for us both. ( crying) We love you, mis ninas. We love you so much.

Steve:

I love you, ladies. Have fun.

The recording shuts off and Santiago takes the laptop, deactivating the device, and waits for the ladies to stop crying before speaking.

Santiago:

(reaching into his briefcase, coming out with an eight-inch box) 'Nita, he said you'd get a kick out of this.

Anita opens the box, and laughs as she pulls the same knife from the box, that Steve playfully threatened to cut Paulo's genitals off with.

Santiago:

And, he left you both this. (He slides her a plain white envelope.)

Anita opens the envelope, extracting a check, and, upon examining it, her bottom lip drops as she places her free hand over her now open mouth.

Santiago:

Now, there's a few things you should know about that money. That check can't be cashed until July 27 of this year, your eighteenth birthday. Once you cash it, 10 percent will automatically go to me, it's my fee, plus, I had to find you in order to get paid. That was the only way your father and I could make sure that you got the money, and for him to know that I wouldn't steal it all. And, lastly, once you cash it, you two need to report to the Municipal Building. I had to have you two passports and papers made, you two just have to take the photographs. And, you two have first-class plane tickets ready for you, you need only pick a destination. And, Princess gets $1 million, a trust fund, when she turns eighteen.

She hugs Anabella.

Anita:

So, you get $1 million automatically?

Santiago:

As soon as you cash that check on your eighteenth birthday, it'll automatically come to my account. What your father and I did couldn't've happened without his signature, and you made it extremely easy for me to find you, once you got that ID last week. So, do you know where you two would like to go?

Anita:

Cali, Colombia.

Act 11-Scene 34: July 27, 2011. 7 A.M.

Divino-Te Deseo Lo Mejor plays throughout this montage as Anita and Anabella stand outside of a bank, with a man in a suit, as three of them wait patiently as one of two security guards unlocks the doors to the bank.

Male:

Miss Jerez-Davis, you know this isn't protocol?

301

Anita:

I know that, but, I'm trying to run away from sex-traffickers, and, I promise you, once you see why I'm having you do this for me, I'll make it worth you guys time.

The security guard unlocks the door, and…

Fade to the banker looking at a computer screen, Anita and Anabella seated across from him. He examines the document, along with her ID, presses the Return key, and the screen changes, showing $10,100,000 dollars exactly. Right below that a deposit block shows $1,010,000 going to an offshore account, belonging to one.

Banker:

Santiago Santos, you're aware—

Anita:

—Yes, I'm aware. Ten percent.

He nods confirmation.

Banker:

You're also aware that, one Anabella Jerez-Davis (nodding toward Anabella), I'm guessing that's her, there, gets $1 million on her eighteenth birthday, November 13, 2020? So, you can only spend so much of this money.

Anita:

Si.

Banker:

How much will you be taking out today?

Anita:

Our parents made flight reservations for us, first class. I'd like to change that to a private jet rental, to Cali, Colombia, flying today. And, give us a hundred thousand dollars.

Banker:

So, subtract the private jet from the $8,990,000?

Anita:

(smiling) Yes.

Show her giving the banker and the two security guards small stacks of 100-dollar bills.

Show Anita and Anabella both getting their picture taken, which appear on passports, listing Jerez-Davis as their last names, getting stamped and handed to Anita.

Show the two sisters on the private jet, eating a feast, laughing and drinking orange juice from champagne glasses. Show Anita staring out of the window, while Anabella runs around, playing with a stewardess.

Anita:

Ana, come see how pretty the ocean looks with me.

Anabella goes to her sister, kisses her cheek.

Anabella:

Happy Birthday, hermana.

Anita:

Thank you, mi amor. It's Mama and Papa's anniversary, too.

Anabella:

Happy Anniversary, Mama and Papa.

Anita:

Happy Anniversary.

Fade to a map, showing them arrive in Cali, Colombia.

Scene 35-3:34 P.M.: Anabella holds Anita's left hand as they both stare at something, both have tears falling from their eyes.

The camera swings behind them, showing the house they used to live in slightly renewed, but still the same.

Inside, a grandmother, her son and his wife, who holds a baby, while his little boy and girl, stare at the two strange girls outside their window, crying. The lady holding the baby says...

Wife:

It's the girl from the portrait!

Husband:

Oh, my God! That is her! The Bloody Bride and Groom's daughter!

Grandmother:

Go let them in.

The husband goes and opens the door, shocking Anita and Anabella, causing them to dry their eyes.

Husband

We know who you are. You used to live here, didn't you?

Anita:

Yes, how'd you know that?

Husband:

Come in, and I'll show you.

Anabella and Anita walk nervously toward the door and enter. The husband closes the door behind them, and begins the introductions-

Carlos:

I'm Carlos. This is my mother, Yanina; my wife, Rosa; our new baby, Juan; and our two little ones, Maria and David—they're three and five.

Anita and Anabella both greet the children who shy away nervously, then the grandmother, who smiles at Anita, rubs Anabella's face. Then they both go and admire the baby as the husband walks down the hallway.

Rosa:

Would you like to hold him?

Anita:

( barely containing her excitement) Can I?!

Rosa hands her Juan, and Anita lightly bounces him.

Anita:

He's so precious.

Rosa:

Gracias.

Anabella:

I want to hold him.

The ladies all laugh.

Anita:

You have to sit down, hermana.

Anabella hurries to the couch and holds her arms out, to the amusement of the women. Anita slowly hands her Juan.

Anita:

Hold his head, Ana, be careful.

Anabella:

Okay. (Once he settles into her embrace, she looks up, smiling.) He's so cute.

Rosa:

Thank you, Ana.

Carlos enters the room with a box in one arm, and the portrait of the Jerez-Davis family gripped in the other hand. He sets the box down and turns the painting toward the group.

Carlos:

This is how we knew who you were.

Anita walks slowly to the portrait, drops to her knees, and breaks down immediately, touching her and Sonrisa's faces on the portrait softly, then Steve's and her brother's. Anabella cries and hands Juan back to his mother, and kneels behind her sister, wrapping her arms around her shoulders, and putting her left cheek, on Anita's right, both staring at the portrait through teary eyes.

Carlos and his family bunch together, letting the two sisters cry it out.

Carlos:

If it makes you two feel any better, your parents are legends, folk heroes, even. The Bloody Bride and Groom. The only two people who've ever challenged Vibora. They killed thirty something guards to get to Vibora before they killed him. People love your parents. Of course, another drug lord sprouted up, but, they got the Snake. I couldn't believe it when we bought the house. When the realtor first showed us this house, and we saw that portrait, my mother demanded that I buy it. She said it just felt nice in here for some reason.

Yanina:

Vibora and his father, who I grew up under, caused so much pain, your parents did Colombia a great service killing the Snake.

Carlos:

They say they chose today, July 27, because it was their anniversary. Is that true?

Anita:

(staring blankly at the portrait) Si.

Carlos:

That's how they came up with the names 'The Bloody Bride and Groom.'

Anita:

It's also my birthday. They got married on my fifteenth birthday.

Carlos:

WOW!!! I wish I could've been at that party. (He hands her the box.) I think this belongs to you.

Anita looks into the box, and, the first thing she lays eyes on is her Miss Colombiana sash, which she grabs, clutching it to her chest. She has a quick flashback.

Flashback:

(visualizing) Steve places the sash over her shoulders. She and Steve dance at the Wedding/Quinceañera .

She touches Steve's face on the portrait, remembering.

Anita:

I wish you could've been there, too. It was the best day of my life.

Scene 36:10:17 P.M.-Chosen Few ft. Omega & Coscuella-Latin Girl plays throughout the scene.

Various shots flash in a rapid montage:

Show a lady leading an unidentified man down a hotel hallway by his tie, smiling at him coquettishly.

Show a liquor bottle going up, coming down, as the lady takes it from him, takes a drink herself, and kisses him.

Show the lady straddling him as he looks up at her topless form, bare breasts swinging in his face as she cuffs his wrists to the bedpost. She places his penis into her mouth, bobbing up and down momentarily, looking at her date seductively. His head pops up as he notices her putting her short and flimsy top back on, reaching for his pants, extracts his wallet, takes all of the money, and knocks on the bathroom door.

Once it opens, a little girl steps out first, followed by an older girl.

ANITA!!!

She grabs her purse, reaches into it, coming out with a roll of bills, peels off five of them, and pays the hooker. As the prostitute turns to exit, Anita stops her as she admires Paulo, peels off three more bills, hands them to the hooker, who exits, pulling her too short skirt down, which does nothing at all.

Anita:

Paulo.

Paulo looks as scared as a deer running from a wolf pack. Anita rushes to him, gently stroking his face. She kisses his cheek.

Anita:

( toying with him) Paulo, mi amor, you don't look too happy to see me. (sticking her tongue into his right ear, massaging his balls and stroking his member) Remember when you violated me on my porch right after you watched me and my mother get raped? God rest her soul. Kiss me, Paulo. (She pulls his face toward her, forcefully.) I said kiss me, fucking faggot!!! Or I will kill you!!!

Paulo turns to her, reluctantly, and hesitantly kisses her as he watches an angry Anabella turn the portrait of their family around to be seen by Paulo.

Anita:

Don't take your eyes off of that painting until I tell you to! Now, don't worry about my sister seeing your parts. Unfortunately, thanks to you, she's seen many things that she should never have seen. Thanks to you, cowards, we both know what it feels like to be captives in a bordello, just like my mother was her entire life under Vibora. Two men saw my little sister and tried to rape her in Spain. ( visualizing as she speaks) I clawed the first man's eyes out, and, stabbed the second man so many times in the neck, that I damn near decapitated him. She's all I have, now, and, from beyond the grave, my father rescued us from that hell you sold us into.

Paulo:

Nita, I—

Anita:

Shut the fuck up, swine!!! You better not say another word, coward!!! I will kill you!!!

Anita talks to him as she reaches down by the bedpost, by his right foot, coming up with a pair of handcuffs, which she dangles in the air, taunting him. He moves his leg away from her.

Anita:

Tsk, tsk, tsk, tsk, papi. I thought you'd react this way.

She walks to her purse, and pulls out a sheathed knife, the same knife Steve left her, unsheathes it, and turns to Anabella, who eagerly runs to her.

Anita:

Take this and press it against that bastard's neck. If he so much as whimpers, or doesn't comply, you drag it across his fucking throat hard and fast. Besame.

The sisters peck quickly, and Anabella runs toward Paulo, putting the knife under his chin, pressing it against his neck, drawing a little blood. Anita sees his underwear, grabs them from the floor, and charges Paulo, stuffing as much of them as will fit into his mouth.

Anita:

Bastard!!!

She grabs his leg, he jerks, Anabella starts to slice.

Anita:

No, bella. He's getting the message. ( She cuffs his right foot to the post, then cuffs his left to its post.) Ana, bring me the knife.

Anabella snaps the knife up his right cheek, opening it, before she walks to her sister and hands her the weapon. Anita kisses her cheek.

Anita:

You know that wasn't very nice, mi amor.

Anabella:

He's a fucking animal!

Anita:

( looking at Paulo) She's no fan of yours, papi, you dirty, greedy son-of-a-bitch! If you had only waited, and not sold us for thousands, if only you had truly loved me as I loved you, and been our protector like my father was to our mother, you could've had millions, Paulo. He left us millions!!! That's how we were able to escape the sex-traffickers. And, most importantly, how I was able to get back to beautiful Cali, to visit the man who sold my sister and I to filthy pimps! ( She raises the knife, showing it to Paulo.) I know you remember this particular knife, don't you, papi?

Paulo has a horrified flashback, and it shows in his wide-eyed look.

Flashback:

Show Steve grabbing Paulo by the collar, telling him to pull his dick out.

Anita:

(chuckling) Yeah, you remember this knife. So, you must remember what my papa wanted to cut with it, don't you?

Paulo squirms. Pathetic. Anita massages his scrotum.

312

Anita:

It's no use, papi. There was a time when I would've gladly put these balls in my mouth for you. Now, I'm going to put them in yours. A fitting birthday gift for me, and a wonderful gift for mi papa on he and my mother's anniversary. It's funny, but, I thought my father was just joking about cutting your dick and balls off, but, after seeing him start a war with the most powerful Drug Lord in Colombia, over my mother, and, after Vibora killed my brothers, the Bloody Bride and Groom hungrily sought vengeance; not only do I now know he would've approved of me cutting your balls off for what you did to his Beauty Queen and Princess, I feel as if I'd be doing him a disservice, if I didn't cut your balls off. You don't deserve to live, or breed, if you don't bleed out. But, I'm tired of talking to you, now. You get the picture. So, without further ado. (She grips his scrotum, tightly, squeezing on purpose, causing him to scream into his underwear.) This is for my brothers, mother ( looking down on him menacingly), and mi padre!

He screams as she slices his balls clean off and a stream of blood flows quickly.

Fade to black

Prophex-Mi Muneca plays throughout the closing credits

# About the Author

Email address: anointhimking@gmail.com

Ronni Curry a.k.a. King Tremayne, resides in Las Vegas, Nevada. Single, no kids, enjoying life.

**BEWARE OF THE FOLLOWING BOOKS BY RONNI CURRY**

Poetry-
I Came, I Saw, I Wrote
I'm At You All
The Charm

Screenplays-
Don't Get Involved
Nothin' But The Truth
Hit Man Hit
Pay Close Attention
Return of The KKK
The Devil Himself
Anarchy
U.N.C. University of North Controversy
U.N.C. ME AGAIN
U.N.C. ON 3!!!
Mi Latina

Philosophy-
The Holy Manifesto

Screenplay Still To Come-
The Elementalls Parts 1-3